P9-EDM-960

NO MARBLE ANGELS

Short Fiction

NO MARBLE ANGELS

Joanne Leedom-Ackerman

TC
WP

TEXAS
CENTER
FOR
WRITER'S
PRESS

First Edition

©1985 by Joanne Leedom-Ackerman
Printed in the United States of America

Texas Center for Writers Press, Inc.
P.O. Box 428
Montrose, Alabama 36559

ISBN 0-916092

ACKNOWLEDGMENTS

Thank you to the friends,
teachers, and family who have
encouraged my work and been a
part of these stories.
Special thanks to my mother
for her generosity of spirit,
to my father for his exactitude,
to my husband Peter to whom this book is dedicated,
to my agent Jane Wilson of JCA Literary Agency,
to friend and poet Clayton Eshleman,
to friends in the New York writing
group who were the first audience and
critics for several of these stories,
to Janice White, an early editor of my work,
to James P. White, a caring writer,
friend, and publisher and to
The Texas Center for Writers Press.

To my husband Peter
for his love and vision

TABLE OF CONTENTS

The stories in this collection were written over a span of fifteen years and revised continuously. "No Marble Angels," "The Tutor," and "Of Imagination" are excerpts from a novel yet to be published.

NO
MARBLE
ANGELS

Raleigh, 1968

The night offered no sign of an emergency. Shannon Douglas lay sleeping under a white cotton canopy in front of an open window. Light broke apart on the carpet in her room, shifting as the moon shifted. Outside wisteria vines stirred in the shadows, and the room smelled of the sweet dense flower. She slept with the covers pulled back in a blue-flowered gown. One arm stretched above her head as though she were reaching in her sleep, but her body lay motionless. As the moon crossed the arc of the sky and began its descent, the phone beside her bed rang. Next door a dog barked. Between the sounds Shannon began and awakened from a dream.

Downstairs Wes Douglas answered the phone from the couch in his study where he had fallen asleep. The television still murmured in the corner, and a reading light burned into his eyes.

Shannon and her father met on the landing after the call. It had been her aunt on the phone. Rheba, her maid, had been stabbed. Her uncle had gone to the hospital; her cousin was still out on a date, and her aunt was alone and afraid. Shannon grabbed the car keys from the hall table and a Middlebury College sweatshirt from a brass hook. "Let's go."

Her father hesitated as if he wanted to say something to her, but she was already at the door. Her thin mouth was set in a defensive line; the look bid him away. She opened the door. She didn't want him to speak for she knew he

1

didn't know what to say. As if realizing this himself, he picked up his wallet and without a word followed her outside. Honeysuckle and gardenias perfumed the night air. In the mimosa trees whippoorwills trilled; the crickets chirped. The moonlight settled in a filigree across the lawn.

Shannon and her father sped in the blue Lincoln Continental the few blocks to her aunt's house in silence. At the door Josie Simpson Douglas met them in a bathrobe with the shiny remains of night cream over her face. She led them to the kitchen where she'd set out coffee and cookies as though she'd invited them to a party. She brought in napkins, put down plates, poured cream. Her hands searched for activity as she chatted in an excited drawl. Yet behind her liveliness, a startled, betrayed look flickered in her eyes.

"I've never heard anything like it," she said filling cups with coffee. "Screams like a cat fornicating or dying. It frightened Joe and me so that we sat straight up in bed. Joe turned on the light till we realized it was coming from out back and whoever it was might see us. We turned off the light then and went to the window where we saw Rheba in the doorway of her quarters holding a knife. Joe thought she was hurt, but we were afraid to go down. Then Rheba started towards the house still carrying the knife. She began hitting at the kitchen door. I hurried to see if the noise had wakened Georginna, and that's when I saw she wasn't even home. I thought of her still out there and of what might happen."

"What happened to Rheba?" Shannon urged. Her green eyes pressed upon her aunt. Her small nose flared as it did when she grew excited.

Josie took a swallow of coffee. "Rheba was pounding on the glass. In the back porch light she looked like a crazy woman. I was almost afraid to let her in, but Joe saw she was all covered with blood. He called an ambulance while I tried to clean her up the best I could, but she was hurt pretty bad. I can't imagine who would have done such a thing. I wonder what she did."

"Why do you think she did anything?" Shannon asked.

2

Josie reached for a macaroon. She was a tall, husky woman, and her uncorseted body slouched in the chair. "Shannon, honey, someone doesn't come in and practically kill you for no reason. To rob you maybe, but if they were going to rob, why wouldn't they have broken into our house? Rheba doesn't have anything."

Shannon lifted the china cup to her lips. She didn't answer. She stared into her aunt's face; it was a kind face, grown complacent over the years. She tried to remember her talk with Rheba just this afternoon. Today had been her first Sunday home in almost a year, her first since she'd graduated from college. They'd had a family dinner, and afterwards she'd lingered at the table stacking plates to take into the kitchen. As always the table had been set with a pink linen cloth, bone china, heavy Georgian silver: a fork for salad, one for the main course, one for dessert, two spoons and two or three knives. At the end of dinner half the silver was left because everyone except Aunt Josie used the same fork for salad as for roast beef and the same knife to cut the meat as they used to butter the rolls. Shannon had gathered the clutter of silverware and gold-rimmed dessert plates and backed through the kitchen door.

"I was thinking you better come out and say whatsfor," Rheba said from the sink where she was rinsing the plates.

"Hey, Rheba..." Shannon went over and hugged her. Rheba was a wiry woman who moved furniture and hefted baskets of wet laundry, but today she'd felt frail in Shannon's arms. Rheba had helped raise her, along with Aunt Josie, ever since her mother died ten years ago, before that even. She'd spent as much time in Rheba's kitchen and Aunt Josie's screened porch as she had in her own home for as long as she could remember.

"Been home over a week and hadn't even come by to say hello," Rheba complained. "That's not like you, Shannon. You got a reason or you just been plain neglectful?" Shannon stacked the plates Rheba had rinsed into the dishwasher. She avoided Rheba's eyes. "Even yor friends starting to complain... that old boyfriend Brandt whats-his-name, he called here, say he tried you at your house time and again, but you never will call him back."

"I've been busy," Shannon said.

"We all busy." Rheba's pinched brown face peered at her. "Georginna say you coming home just to leave again; no sense getting too attached to you. But I say it's time you stayed for a while. Yor daddy for one needs you about." Rheba handed her a plate.

"What's wrong with Daddy?"

"Nothin wrong with him. He just needs his chile around; that's all."

"He's never even home."

"You two still strangers to each other, aren't you?"

Shannon didn't answer. She shut the dishwasher, turned the knob, then listened to the hot water rush across the dishes.

Rheba had always gotten to the heart of what troubled her. When she was a child she used to sit at the kitchen table and help Rheba shell peas or fold laundry and wait for Rheba to unravel what bothered her. Sometimes she didn't even know herself what it was, but Rheba could circle it, untangling the knots until she finally drew it out...whether it was a friend who had slighted her or her father who had ignored her or her mother who had suddenly died on her...Rheba would find the loneliness and soothe it until it receded.

"It is unusual for someone to attack a maid for no reason in this neighborhood," her father was saying. He folded his hands behind his head. His peppered grey hair was stylishly cut. His eyes were cautious as he spoke.

Josie began telling him all they could have stolen, had they broken into the main house, when the front door opened. "Georginna?" she called.

But Joe Douglas stepped into the doorway. A stocky, muscular man with a flushed face and thinning hair, he wore soiled pants, a Banlon shirt and a cap. He lacked the polished appearance of his younger brother, but his eyes were sharp.

"You mean Georginna's still not home? I can't understand what came over you, Josie, letting a young girl like that go out with a twenty-two year old man." He dragged into the room. "Wes ...Shannon."

"I called them," Josie said. "I got afraid after you left.

How's Rheba?"

Joe shook his head. "We better start looking for a new maid."

Josie gasped.

"Whoever did it, hurt her pretty bad. She may be in the hospital a long time."

Josie glanced at Shannon, who stared intently at her uncle. "We'll do whatever we can of course," Josie offered, "whatever she's done."

Joe sat down at the table. "I don't see what we can do. She could be in the hospital for months, the doctor said. She didn't carry any insurance. It's beyond me why she never bought any. I must have talked with her a dozen times about it. We just can't swing thousands of dollars in hospital bills right now. I told her not to worry in the ambulance; she was all upset at how much it was going to cost, but frankly I told the doctor as soon as she was stable to transfer her to the county hospital. The best thing we can do is get her whatever she's entitled to from the government—unemployment, disability—and get her in with the county; then I guess we could pick up any cost left over."

Joe reached to the pantry and poured brandy into the coffee Josie passed him. "I thought about it all the way home. Rheba would understand. We'll store her things in the garage, and when she gets out, she can come back, but until then, you better start looking for a maid."

"But Rheba is family," Shannon declared.

Josie's thick-lidded eyes turned slowly to her. "Rheba is not *our* family," she said. "She is like family, but she is not family."

Shannon stood. She went to the sink where she looked out the window. The back porch lights were on, and she stared at the clapboard quarters beside the garage. Wisteria hung in heavy purple clusters over the porch by Rheba's room. Rheba had lived in that room five days a week for the last twenty-five years. She had a son Shannon's age, who lived with her mother across town where Rheba lived the other two days of the week. She had been almost forty when

5

she had Washington. Josie agreed to let her stay on, but there wasn't room for a baby in the servant's quarters so Rheba had her son and came back to work two weeks later without the child. No one but Rheba knew who the father was.

"*Do you and Washington still talk?*" *Shannon had asked Rheba this afternoon.*

Rheba paused from rinsing the knives and forks. She pushed her grey hair off her face with the back of her hand. "We don't see so much of each other anymore, but I know when something troubling his mind. It used to be I could get him to tell me what it was." Her shoulders sagged in her white uniform, and her top lip tucked under the way Shannon remembered it did when something was worrying her. "But Washington calling himself Malik these days."

"Does that bother you?"

Rheba spread out a dish towel and began laying the silverware on it. "The name don't bother me so much. I don't much like the name Malik, but then I never like the name Washington either. That was my mamma's idea, and since she the one raising him most of the time, I let her name him." She spread another towel on the counter and began washing the long-stem crystal goblets which she handed one by one to Shannon.

"But Washington in with friends I don't think much of; they too sure of theirselves. I always trusted Washington long as he follow his heart, but he listens to other people now. Looks at me living in one room all my life serving white folks and wonders what I got to teach him. I guess I wonder sometimes too." Rheba set the last two goblets on the towel.

"It's odd," Shannon said.

"What's that?"

"You taught me my whole life, but it doesn't count. Washington holds it against you; Uncle Joe and Aunt Josie don't even know it. And I'll go off somewhere because I don't fit here. I wanted to come back and find this was my home, but it's not."

Rheba's dark eyes narrowed. Her lips closed over teeth which were too big for her mouth. She began folding the towel with quick fingers, pressing the creases to the corner. "Well, Shannon Marie Douglas, you have got yourself educated beyond me at last if this

6

ain't your home."

"Have you called her son?" Shannon asked.

"Washington?" I wouldn't have the first idea how to get hold of Washington," Josie answered.

"I'm sure he'd like to know."

"If I knew how to phone him, I would, but I don't think he even has a phone. The last number I had for them was disconnected a while ago."

Shannon grew silent. She turned and stared back out the window. Her eyes focused on the morning glory vines twisting up the side of Rheba's room. Their blue and purple trumpets were closed for the night. They would open in the gentle light of dawn but would fold again in the heat of mid-day. She moved to the stove and poured herself another cup of coffee. She stared at the pale red coil of the electric range then looked down at the clean tiles of her aunt's kitchen. She drank the coffee with her back to her family, holding the cup so tightly in her hand that she was afraid it might break. Yet she was even more afraid to set it down and turn to face her family for she was afraid then she would cry.

The front door opened, and a soft, lilting voice whispered, "Sh-h-h...it's upstairs." The family in the kitchen grew quiet. Joe and Josie looked at each other; then Joe stood, and Josie followed. The hall light flashed on. "Just where the hell do you think you're going, young man?" Joe demanded.

Shannon and her father moved to the edge of the doorway where they saw Georginna and Brandt Phillips halfway up the stairs, hand in hand.

"Daddy! Mama! What are you doing up? Are you spying on me?"

"We're not the ones answering questions," Joe retorted. "You come down right now, and you too, sir." Joe looked at his watch. "I want to hear where you've been, and what you're doing getting home at a quarter till two in the morning. And why were you taking a young man upstairs with you?"

"I'm not a child, Daddy. You have no right to interrogate me." Georginna drew up her small shoulders. She was wearing a sun dress, and both straps had fallen off her shoulders. Her hair was tangled; her eyes, puffy, and her lips, smeared.

"I'm your father, and I have every right. But first I want to question this young man."

"Mamma!" Georginna pleaded. "Daddy, you will not. You don't have to answer, Brandt." Her words slurred, and she was leaning on the staircase for support. Then she saw Shannon and her uncle in the doorway. "Uncle Wes! Shannon! My god, did you call the police too? I can't believe you came, Shannon."

Brandt glanced over at Shannon and smiled. He and Shannon had dated in high school, and he seemed pleased to have her here as a witness, but Shannon's eyes were focused on her cousin.

"For your information, Georginna, the reason Uncle Wes and Shannon are here has nothing to do with you," Josie said. "Rheba's been stabbed tonight, and they came over to give us comfort which is more than we can say for you."

"Rheba?" Georginna looked at Shannon. "Where? When?"

Josie told Georginna what had happened, and Georginna sank down onto the stairs. She stared at the floor in front of her; then all of a sudden her tiny shoulders heaved forward, and she vomited all over the peach carpet and over Brandt Phillips' shiny leather loafers. Brandt looked stunned as his eyes moved from his shoes to Georginna. Shannon saw in them the urge to bolt. She doubted her uncle saw the same urge, but he had the same idea for he opened the front door. "Perhaps it's time you left," he said. And Brandt, without further prompting, without glancing back at Georginna or Shannon or anyone, took the invitation and disappeared into the night as fast as his soiled shoes could take him.

On the way home that morning, in the twelve blocks between Williamson Drive and St. Mary's Street, in the first lighting of the sky, Shannon decided to tell her father she was moving to New York at the end of the summer. She had been postponing the decision for months. When she entered her father's study that evening, he was sitting with his feet up on his desk contemplating a map of the northside. He was dressed in a three-piece grey suit; his face was tanned by a sun lamp, and he was, even in his daughter's eyes, a handsome man.

"Did you call the hospital today?" he asked.

"They say she can have visitors in a day or so after she's moved." Shannon leaned her pale arms onto the desk. "Daddy, I've been doing a lot of thinking," she began without transition, "and I think I'm going to take the fellowship in New York. First of all, Columbia offers me more money than Duke..."

Her father fixed a pin into the map then looked up. "The money isn't important."

"And Charlotte, you remember Charlotte..."

"The one you spent last Christmas with." His voice still registered disapproval.

"That's right. She's gotten a job in New York and an apartment, and she's looking for a roommate."

"You're going to Columbia because Charlotte needs a roommate?"

"Columbia happens to be an excellent university."

"Isn't Duke an excellent university?" He set the map down and lowered his feet to the floor.

Duke was only half an hour away. "Duke is a good school," she conceded. She wished her father would argue with her the way Uncle Joe did rather than stopping at the edge of his disapproval as if he didn't dare go further. "I also know a lot of people in New York," she went on.

"You know a lot of people in Raleigh-Durham."

She shifted on the chair. Outside the sunlight had faded into the shadows of the garden. The warm air drifted through the french doors. "I've been thinking about this a long time, and it just seems best."

Her father considered her answer. He leaned towards

her. "Have you thought about what sort of men you'll meet at Columbia? I know that's not the only consideration, but it's one you don't seem to think about."

She picked up a pen and began to mark on a Douglas Realty notepad. "I think about it."

"What sort are they?"

"I don't know. I'm not going to graduate school to catch a man."

"I'm not saying you are. I simply asked what sort of men you were likely to meet at a place like Columbia?"

"All kinds I expect." She pushed a strand of dark hair from her eyes. She had wide eyes, a small nose, a fine mouth. Her face held the possibility of beauty, but she took little pains with herself. She set down the pen and met her father's gaze. All her life people had told her how much she looked like her father, but she didn't see the resemblance. She saw only how different they were. Yet because she was insecure about men, his view threatened her, and a defiant, vulnerable look now settled over her face.

Her father glanced away. Ever since she'd come home he'd been seeing her mother in her. "Maybe I am out of place trying to give you advice," he said finally. "You always do what you want anyway; I don't guess you're likely to change." From the edge of his desk he picked up a trophy he'd won from the Chamber of Commerce and held it around its base. "But I want you to be happy, honey, I really do."

"I appreciate that, Daddy." She wanted to say that if he didn't have a right to advise her, who did. Part of her wanted him to care enough to give the advice while the other part rebelled at his trying to take responsibility in her life at this late date. "I guess I don't have to decide everything tonight," she retreated. "I still have a little time."

On Wednesday Shannon went to visit Rheba in the county hospital where she'd been moved the day before. Connected to various feeding and disposal devices, Rheba had slept most of the trip across town and had awakened in a large white room behind two white curtains which separated her from the other patients in the room. That afternoon Washington came to see her.

Josie has finally been persuaded by her own uneasiness over what had happened and by her conversation with Shannon to unearth an old address book and look up the last address for Rheba's mother. She wasn't sure if Mrs. Jackson still lived on Heck Street, but she decided she could at least go there. Turning down the half-dirt, half-paved road she recognized the yellow clapboard house and saw Mrs. Jackson and Washington sitting on the porch. Approaching them, she assumed a solemn expression. Carefully she told her story, apologizing for what had happened though she didn't really know what had happened, but apologizing as though it had been her fault, and on the porch that afternoon she felt somehow it had.

Rheba's mother and son only nodded at the news. They didn't ask questions. She emphasized this fact later when she reported the tale of her journey. She had been prepared to stay and tell them everything she'd seen, but they simply thanked her for coming and didn't ask a single question.

"Of course we'll stay in touch," she had assured them and herself as she left. Her whole visit lasted less than five minutes. She drove away quickly for suddenly she'd felt afraid, not of them but of what had transpired between them.

Washington visited Rheba the next day. He only stayed a short time, and after he left, Rheba slept for the rest of the afternoon and well into the night; but at three in the morning she woke up screaming and had to be given a sedative. The day of her move her condition had been listed as serious, but stable.

When Shannon arrived at Wake County the following day, she was shown into Rheba's cubicle by a nurse who walked on tiptoe and told her Rheba had suddenly gotten worse. She had expected Rheba to show the strain of what she'd been through, but she wasn't prepared for the woman she saw. Rheba looked as though she'd aged ten years and lost half her body's weight. She was wrapped in bandages and propped up on pillows. The loose white hospital gown was hunched around her and made her appear even less substantial than she was. Her skin was ashen, and she looked so weak that Shannon couldn't imagine her only a few days earlier carrying a tray of heavy dishes. Rheba's eyes were shut when the nurse drew the curtain aside, and Shannon glanced around to see if she should proceed.

"She's awake," the nurse said. "She's just resting." And at that assurance, Rheba opened her eyes, which began to tear as soon as she saw Shannon.

"Rheba..." Shannon sank into the chair beside her. Rheba's head was bandaged around the forehead. From the bristles of grey hear, Shannon could see that part of her head had been shaved. "We miss you..." she whispered. Rheba didn't answer, and finally Shannon said, "Oh, Rheba, what happened?"

But Rheba just shook her head and shut her eyes. She stretched out her fingers, and Shannon took her hand. Rheba began to breathe heavily for a moment as if she were falling asleep, but again her eyes opened. Finally she spoke, and her voice was stronger than Shannon expected. "They try to kill an old fool," she said.

"Who did?"

"The monkey on they backs. Go get us money from the house, they say."

"Did you know them?"

"Bad ones. Ust hang around the doorstep every weekend I come home see if I brought anything."

"They were Washington's friends?"

Rheba dropped her head back on her pillow. "Washington never they friend, but they hang round anyway."

"They stabbed you because you wouldn't give them Uncle Joe's money?"

Rheba turned her head to the side and fixed her eyes on the wall. "Because I'm an old fool. Old fool pull a butcher knife on two grown men, tell them to get out like they still boys on the stoop. They hyped up on drugs, but they almost go till suddenly I see they not boys, and they see what I see and next thing they got the knife or they own knives, and I feel the blood. I hadn't screamed and Mister Douglas hadn't turned on the light, they'd of kilt me." Rheba shut her eyes. "Maybe it of been the best thing if they had."

"Don't say that." Shannon squeezed her hand and tried to pass her own strength on to Rheba.

But Rheba didn't answer. Again Shannon thought she was falling asleep. Shannon glanced about the space which had been given her. There was only the hospital bed and a white metal cabinet. On top of the cabinet was a box of Kleenex, a Bible and next to these a glass of water with Rheba's teeth in it. Shannon stared at the teeth. They were yellowed and stained; magnified by the water, they looked grotesque. The teeth were so personal and vulnerable that Shannon couldn't take her eyes off them. She had never been so close to Rheba's intimate living before. As a child she had visited Rheba's room by the garage. It was always neat but cluttered with a double bed, an old dresser stacked with magazines, a worn arm chair with a floor lamp arched over it and a wardrobe where Rheba hung her faded dresses and uniforms. It smelled musty and damp, and it was dark for vines hung so thick over the windows that little light could get through. Off the room in a smaller area was a toilet stained yellow and a shower stall and a sink. These two rooms were where Rheba had lived almost half her life. Shannon hadn't been to visit Rheba's room in years.

Rheba sighed now. Shannon looked back at her to see if she was awake. She asked quietly, "Has Washington visited yet?"

Rheba nodded.

"I should go see him," she volunteered. She hadn't seen Washington since high school. She remembered playing with him when she was a little girl. She remembered Rheba's stories about him most of all. She used to love to hear Rheba talk about what a bad boy he was because she knew Rheba was really saying how much she loved him. She would listen to the tales of Washington skipping school and going hunting as though he were some character out of a book. That

13

was about how much reality he had for her. She liked the idea of finding Washington and seeing who he had become.

But Rheba shook her head. "No," she said sharply.

"I'd like to tell him personally how sorry I am and see if there's anything I can do."

Rheba opened her eyes. She stared directly at Shannon now. "He don care how sorry you are. Why should he?" Her voice was harsh.

"But maybe I could do something."

"Nothing you can do. You only make things worse you go there. You stay where you belong."

Shannon didn't understand why Rheba wouldn't let her see her son, but she nodded, "Well, what did he say?"

"Nothing to say. He see what happen. He stood at the foot of the bed, didn't come closer. Mostly he just stare off over my head. When I tell him what happen, all he ask is why I didn give them the money, who I'm protecting?"

"Rheba, I'm sure when Aunt Josie and Uncle Joe find out what really happened..."

"He just keep asking why I didn give them the money, and laying here I'm starting to think he right. I don think he coming back. He don say it, but I can see it in his eyes. He hardened hisself against what happened to me, and he ain't coming back to see it again."

"Rheba, I'm sure he will..." But a nurse came in then and told Shannon it was time to leave. "I'll come back too," she promised, "...tomorrow or the next day." And she leaned over and kissed Rheba on the mouth, something she had never done before, and Rheba's lips felt dry and cold.

Shannon didn't return to the hospital the next day. Instead she began looking for a summer job. That afternoon she stopped by her aunt's house where she found Josie on the screened porch painting landscapes on hollowed out eggs. She donated the eggs to ladies' bazaars around town. Georginna was reading magazines on the divan. No one asked about her visit to Rheba; no one else had visited.

"You'll stay for dinner?" Josie asked, touching a stroke

of yellow to the tiny painting. Shannon nodded. Josie secured the egg in its egg cup then rose to tell the new maid to set an extra place.

As soon as she left, Georginna sat up. "You have got to talk to Mamma," she said. "Daddy's grounded me for *two* weeks and Mamma's agreed."

"Why?" Shannon asked.

"Sh-h-h," Georginna glanced into the living room then gestured for Shannon to follow her up to her bedroom. Inside she locked the bedroom door then dropped onto her bed, her legs crossed, her shoulders rounded in the con-spiratorial pose of a girl at a slumber party sharing gossip about those who weren't there. "Because of the other night. And what's worse, Brandt hasn't called. Has he called you?" She glanced at Shannon from under the thin arch of her eyebrows.

"No."

"Well, I'm sure he was so embarrassed, he'll never call either of us again." She reached over to a shelf lined with dolls and removed one in a frilly crinoline skirt. Lifting the dolls head off, she produced a bottle of scotch. "You want a drink?" She smiled at her cousin's surprise. "You always were more of a prude, Shannon." She poured out a glass.

"Mamma and Daddy still treat me like a child. No one seems to realize I have a lot on my mind these days. Did you know I'm head cheerleader next fall, and my grades have already gone down. Daddy says I'll never get into Duke with grades like last spring. Besides I've even been thinking of going North like you..." she cast a sidelong glance at Shan-non, "...to Middlebury or maybe even Bryn Mawr if I could get in."

There was a knock at the door. "You girls in there?" Josie called. "Georginna, why is your door locked?"

Georginna tucked the bottle back in the doll's skirt. "Just a min...ute..." she answered, handing Shannon the doll to put back on the shelf while Georginna hid her glass. Stuffing a stick of gum into her mouth, Georginna unlocked the door. "I like *some* privacy sometimes you know."

15

"What could be so private?" Josie moved into the room and sat on Georginna's bed as though she were a teenager herself used to sharing secrets with her daughter. She was barefoot and wearing a long flowered muu muu. "What are you two talking about anyway?"

"I was just asking Shannon about college."

"Oh, well, that's good. I've been telling her she should at least apply to Chapel Hill."

"Mamma, I told you..." But before she could repeat what she'd told her mother, the phone rang, and Georginna answered. Glancing at Shannon, she said, "I'll take it in the other room." She handed the phone to her mother. "And hang up and don't listen. She always listens."

"I do not listen," Josie defended as Georginna went out. "She's gotten so high-strung lately..." But when Georginna picked up the extension, Josie paused to hear the other voice.

"She's growing up," Shannon offered.

"That she is. But then you haven't seen her in almost a year what with your working at that camp last summer and spending Christmas in New York. It'll be good for Georginna to have you around for a change, won't hurt anyone, and I can think of a lot of people it might help."

Shannon glanced out the window into the backyard, at the swing set by the hedge, at Rheba's quarters. "I'm not staying in Raleigh, Aunt Josie." She turned and faced her aunt. "Or Durham."

"Why? What's wrong with Raleigh/Durham?"

"Nothing. I just know everyone here and everything here. There are too many places I don't know."

"Places such as?"

"New York. Washington. Baltimore."

"What's in Baltimore? Baltimore's a dirty, smoky city half torn up by riots."

"I don't know what's in Baltimore or anywhere, and I'm never going to know unless I go." Her aunt's double chin tucked in the way it did when she'd heard a friend of hers had said something unkind behind her back. "I wish you wouldn't take this personally," Shannon said. Yet she knew

16

there was no other way for her aunt to take it.

Shannon planned to visit Rheba on Friday, but she finished her job interviews late and went out to dinner with friends instead. However, on Saturday she arrived at the hospital with a handful of carnations. She was feeling more lighthearted than she had since she'd come home. She had several prospects for jobs at community centers, and she was beginning to think she could at least survive Raleigh for the summer. She had come prepared to tell Rheba about the possibilities and talk with her about which job sounded best; but when she pushed back the curtain to Rheba's cubicle, she found the bed empty. The stand beside the bed was empty too. Rheba's teeth were gone; the Bible was gone, and only the box of Kleenex was left. She hurried to the nurse's station on the floor.

"Rheba Jackson?" The nurse looked down at her ledger of patients. "Why, she died Thursday night, dear, passed in her sleep. At her age, in her condition, it was probably for the best."

"What?" Shannon stared at the nurse. Her eyes focused on the plastic supper trays stacked beside her, and she could see the food already congealed.

"I see here that we called her family, and they asked that we take care of the body so it was buried this morning out in the county field. Simple, no marble angels, but I'm sure she would have liked it."

Shannon watched the nurse's placid white face, and she found herself wondering if anyone had put Rheba's teeth in before they buried her. "How do you know?" she asked. "How do you have any idea what she would have liked? I don't know what she would have liked. Her own family didn't know. No one...no one knew what she would have liked."

Shannon turned then and started down the brightly lit corridor; she walked across the newly mopped linoleum, past the janitor mopping the linoleum; and then she began to run, carefully at first so she wouldn't slip, then faster, until she was running as fast as she could as she pushed out the door into the cool, sweet air of the Raleigh summer evening.

THE TUTOR

Baltimore, 1968

The girl did not belong. It was obvious to those watching her walk up Shenandoah Avenue. Under her arm she carried a notebook and a shopping bag. She moved slowly down the street, her eyes darting from side to side — large, curious eyes peering out from under her bangs — observing the squat brick houses, the people on their stoops. Those watching thought perhaps she was a welfare worker making her rounds. Every few steps she glanced into her notebook then again scanned the porches. She smiled, a shy, tentative smile which asked these strangers to smile back at her. It was her smile, her peculiar bidding, which hinted to the neighbors she was not from welfare.

Others watching guessed she was a walker, out soliciting business. Tight jeans. Loose shirt. "Hot tonight, baby, right hot." One of the locals clucked as he sidled up beside her. She glanced at the pavement and walked faster. Hips set high, a little wide, legs long and slim, breasts small under the cotton shirt. She dodged these men like the hockey player she'd been in college, not like a jane on the make. "Hey, green jeans, where you going?" the men called. She flashed a cautious, not-to-be-rude smile then hurried down the block without looking back. On the porches the women, on the street the men watched this white girl passing.

At No. 14 Shenandoah, the girl stopped. She shut her notebook and climbed the broken steps to the porch. She ran her hand around the waist of her slacks, tucking in her shirt; then she brushed fingers through her short dark hair.

19

She started towards the front door but stopped. The house looked empty. The shades were drawn, the windows patched with the *Afro American*. The window frames, swollen past their shape, had been stuffed with rags, and she could see no light inside. On the rotted post which propped up the porch she read a message scrawled in red—"Fuck Them Zoro Lives!"—message scrawled anonymously then covered over with paint by whomever lived there, painted over and over again.

She finally moved to the door and knocked.

Silence.

She knocked again.

From between a chain lock, a face peered out. "Who you?"

"I'm...I'm the tutor." She disliked that word. "I'm Shannon Douglas—is your mother home?"

"Ma-a-a!" the voice shouted down the hall. "That tutor lady's here."

The door shut then opened. She had begun.

Inside, the house fell into shadow. A bare bulb lighted the kitchen at the far end of the hallway. From the living room a tv glowed in one corner and huddled around it two children cast secret glances at the stranger. Furniture jammed close on all sides of them, so much furniture it looked as though the family had gathered everything they could find— lamps, coffee tables, a couch faded brown with stuffing popping through, another couch bright turquoise laminated in plastic, chairs, stools, the shell of a faceless tv—all crowded in this one small room like manna stored up for tomorrow. On top of the television grinned the school pictures of the children, two boys stiff and formal in coats and ties, a girl laughing from behind the frills of a freshly pressed blouse. On the empty tv shell an orange swan filled with plastic daisies coasted among memorabilia, weaving its way among a cowgirl ashtray, an Atlantic City mug, a letter framed in gold. From the wall Jesus smiled down on this family. And next to him Martin Luther King, John Kennedy, and Bobby

Kennedy gazed out from an eternally blue sky stamped in gold: We Shall Overcome.

Slowly Shannon made her way into the hall. The boy who had let her in now stood watching as she came to terms with his home. He towered over her. He stood with his weight shifted to his back foot, his head cocked, his arms folded in front of him. Standing in the shadows he could have been seventeen, eighteen, yet in the light his face showed cheeks still childishly round and a forehead spotted with tiny bumps of teenage acne. His eyes, uncertain, jumped from object to object, not yet sure of how to hold the world with his gaze.

As Shannon passed a cabinet in the hallway, he blocked her path. "That's mine," he said, wedging her between him and the big maple chiffonier. The cabinet's front glass was broken, and on the empty shelves stood a single silver loving cup.

"Oh," she said, not knowing what to say.

"I won it."

"Oh, well, good..."

"I'm going to fill the whole thing with trophies." His eyes scanned the chiffonier then her. "That's what I took it for."

She tried to smile, but instead an anxious, tentative look flitted across her eyes. The boy backed away. His own face tightened, and he began pulling his hair with a large Afro comb. He pointed for her to go to the end of the hallway.

Shannon moved quickly past him; she moved past two bedrooms with mattresses on the floor, past a bathroom, past a closet with a desk in it. While she moved, she studied the objects in these rooms and tried to memorize the pieces of this family's life. As she probed the rooms with her eyes, a woman watched her. An enormous, brooding woman. She sat under a bare light bulb as it swung back and forth over the kitchen table. She sipped water from a jelly jar, and she studied this girl who pried into her home. When Shannon saw the woman, she gave a start; then breaking into an embarrassed smile, she moved quickly towards her. "Hello," she said.

The woman didn't answer. She lifted her large body and straightened it in the chair. Her face was dark and her features, soft and pliant, looked as though they'd been pressed to shape with the palm of a hand in moist clay. Only her eyes stood out distinctly sculpted. She was enveloped in a print housecoat which closed around her like a tent. She stared at Shannon, who shifted uncomfortably under her gaze. The woman looked at the notebook and shopping bag Shannon clutched in her hands. Finally she demanded, "You the tutor?"

"Yes, Shannon...Shannon Douglas." Shannon extended her hand, but Corene Luvurn Roberts just nodded for her to sit down.

"You git here awright?"

"Fine...yes." Shannon settled uneasily into a chair at the table. "Some trouble finding the street sign, that's all."

"That's the boys round here; they twist up them signs for a game." She looked over at her own three children clustered around the tv. "Not mine. They good childrens. That's Tabor, the big one what let you in," she pointed. "Then there's Coretta and Theodore, only folks call them Corry and Bumper. They shy tonight."

The girl uncurled from the floor in the living room. "I ain't shy," she said. "I'm just giving you time to talk to the tutor." She moved into the kitchen. She was only twelve— all arms and legs—but she carried herself like a dancer swaying to a rhythm she alone could hear. Her skin was smooth and dark, and her eyes sparkled like chips of black coral. "You going to teach Ma?" she asked.

"If she wants me to," Shannon said.

"She wants you to awright. You teach me too," she declared. "I'm good at reading, but I can't do science. I'd of made honor roll if I could do science."

Tabor rushed into the kitchen. His eyes darted to Shannon then returned to his sister. "Whatchu mean you'd a made honor roll? You jes dumb thas all." He strutted over to the refrigerator, and as he passed Shannon, he kicked over her bag with his foot. "Ain't nobody teach that girl," he said.

Shannon bent down and started picking up the books.

"Thas so?" Corry challenged. "Least I don't go failin whole grades like some people I know. You see, some people in this family just not too smart."

"Awright you two, go sit and quiet yourselves," Corene said. "They the sassy ones," she apologized.

"I ain't sassy; Tabor is." Corry stuck out her mouth in a pout then turned back to Shannon. "What you goin teach Ma anyway? She goin to finish high school?"

"If she can pass the test," Shannon said.

"Oh, she can pass a test, cain't you, Ma?" Corry turned to her mother.

Corene didn't answer. She sipped water from the jelly jar and stared at the books in Shannon's bag. She reached into a box of starch beside her and began sucking the chalky white powder.

"Ma almost finished high school in Georgia, you know, but then she had to get off the land. That was before I was born. She can get a good job with high school done, can't she?"

Shannon nodded. Corene's eyes narrowed, and her mouth drew tight together. For a moment Shannon thought she was afraid. When Corene saw Shannon watching her, she glanced away and poured out another handful of starch. Slowly she began chewing the powder. Her thoughts like the mass of her flesh formed a wall around her.

"I'm going to college myself," Corry continued. "I'm going to be a teacher or maybe an actress."

"You ain't going to no college, girl." Tabor was up. "Only one make it to college round here is me. I'm the one going to college while you work to support me."

"No girl got sense 'd support you, cept maybe some empty-haided girl like Marcy Johnson. Tabor love Marcy," Corry taunted. Tabor lunged at Corry, but she jumped away, and Tabor went crashing into the table.

"Tabor Roberts! You go sit down 'fore I hit you!" Corene grabbed his arm.

"But Ma, it was Corry's fault..." Tabor protested.

"I don't want to hear no fault. I got eyes, don't I? You boths go sit."

"Cain't I lissen?" Tabor dropped into a chair across from Shannon. "I want to know how long she thinks it be before you pass that test?" He stared at Shannon, serious now. He began fingering her notebook in the middle of the table.

"I don't know, Tabor," she said.

"Ma's smart, you know. Well, she is. She's finished eleventh grade. I expect she should pass that test this year." His tone was suddenly businesslike. He pulled Shannon's notebook to him and started studying the writing inside as though it were the ledger for his family. "She's smart...yes, I expect she'll pass this year," he repeated.

"Ma's going to do computers," Corry interjected. "We're going to get a car maybe...or were you going to be a secretary. I forgot." Corry glanced at her mother. "When we get enough, we'll get a car, maybe even a house outside the city."

"She'll pass this year," Tabor said again, his words part question this time.

"Yes, well, it's possible. I mean I don't know why not," Shannon said, letting herself get swept up into their mood of possibilities. She took a pencil and scribbled something down in the notebook. "Yes, a key punch operator maybe. She could begin there really and move on up." Tabor and Corry grinned at each other. Shannon scribbled something else down. "Or she could be a secretary. If she's good in English and spelling, she could begin there and work into business. Jobs are starting to open..."

All at once Corene shoved up from the table; her chair crashed to the floor. She glared at Shannon. Her face was so angry, Shannon thought for an instant she was going to hit her. "Don't say what you don't know!" she ordered. "Don't make them promises; you don't know that." Her words rebuked them, and suddenly the mood shriveled like a balloon released before tied, its possibilities of flight sucked out and left limp on the pavement. "You can't promise what

24

you don't know," she repeated.

Shannon stared up at her. "I...you're..." she stammered. Tabor and Corry implored her with their eyes. "But if you've finished eleventh grade..." Shannon tried. "I know it was a long time ago, but..." Corene's eyes would not soften. Shannon shifted in a chair. A torn piece of vinyl from the seat dug into her leg. Corene watched her, but Tabor and Corry wouldn't look now. Tabor began pulling at his hair with his comb; Corry fingered a burned piece of formica peeling off the table. Shannon ran her fingers up and down the edge of the notebook. "I mean I don't *really* know," she said. "I don't *know*."

"That's right," Corene said, sitting back down.

As Shannon started pulling books out of her shopping bag, Corene's eyes and mouth again tensed. She looked quickly from Shannon to Tabor to Corry. "Which ones of these would you like to read?" Shannon asked. She spread *A Tale of Two Cities, Huckleberry Finn, Great Expectations, Charlotte's Web* on the table, along with workbooks whose grade levels had been blocked out. The tattered books lay in front of Corene, an army of words to be conquered. But Corene wasn't looking at the books; her eyes had frozen on her children. She was afraid of something. Shannon saw that now.

"You git," she ordered Tabor and Corry. Her words came sharp.

"But Ma..." Corry protested.

"Git!" she demanded.

"Ma..." Tabor argued, but Corene would not relent. Tabor and Corry rose from the table. Slowly they moved towards the living room. From an overstuffed armchair in the corner, Bumper uncurled. He had been sitting there unnoticed the whole time, watching, silently taking in the scene. When Shannon smiled at him, he looked away. Instead he turned towards his mother, his own eyes wary, questioning. Corene just nodded, and he rolled out of the chair and went to join his brother and sister in front of the tv.

Corene poured out another palmful of starch. She licked

25

the dusty white powder as she began to look through the books on the table. She picked up *A Tale of Two Cities* and turned it over and over in her hand. She fingered the worn corners. "A lot of people've read this book," she said. Shannon nodded. She opened the cover slowly and studied the first page. She turned to the back of the book and studied the last page. Then she flipped to the middle. Finally she pulled out a pair of wire glasses from the folds of her housecoat and put them on and studied the book some more. She looked up at Shannon, her face studious, her eyes narrowed. When Shannon smiled at her, Corene turned away. Staring at the cover one last time, she shut the book and shook her head.

She began searching through the other books, her fingers large and brown roaming this small second-hand library. She picked up *Great Expectations,* stared at the title, then put it down without even opening the cover. She looked at the pictures on each of the books—a spider weaving its web, a boy with a fishing pole, a lady knitting at the guillotine. Finally she opened a workbook—level 9—and started turning pages. Her mouth began to form sounds, random words: "think" ... "fall" ... soft full lips barely whispering ... "before" ... "today" ... The words fell out slowly. Shannon watched, hopeful, but Corene closed the book. She didn't look at Shannon this time but quickly picked up another book, then another.

From the living room, her children peered out at her. Shannon glanced over at them, and they began whispering like guilty conspirators. Tabor loudly cleared his throat, and Corry and Bumper darted around and pretended to watch tv. Corene didn't see the children, however. She was sipping water from the jelly jar and staring hard into another book.

" 'Do you want a friend, Wilbur?' " Her words again came slow, but steady this time, her voice rising full. " 'But I can't see you,' said Wilbur jumping to his feet. " 'Go to sleep. You'll see me in the morning...' " Corene glanced up smiling for an instant; then she grew serious again. "I'll take this one," she said.

Shannon looked at the book and tried to smile. *Charlotte's Web.* Fourth grade, maybe fifth. Corene was reading below Corry even. "Good...well, that's good. That's a fine book," Shannon said. "You read well."

Corene's eyes looked at the book then at Shannon. "Don't lie," she said.

"I'm not. I..."

"I don't read good so why say different?"

"You'll get better of course."

"I'm not finishing high school this year," she said flatly, watching Shannon's face.

"Well, probably it will take longer," Shannon tried. Shannon glanced again at Corry and Tabor; their faces were intent on the television now. Only Bumper watched from the corner.

"I can't tell the childrens that." Shannon nodded without speaking. "I'm going to be frank with you," Corene said. "I tole the childrens I finished eleventh grade so they finish themselves. Kids do what their folks do. I quit eighth." She looked into the jelly jar as she talked. "I don't want them to think their ma's stupid. Corry asks help for her work an I cain't help and she say, 'Mamma, you 'spose know how t' do this. Why don you learn?' Now I have to learn first. Then I can teach it to them."

Shannon just nodded. "We'll work hard," she said.

Corene nodded back. She picked up *Charlotte's Web* and began to read, " 'My name,' said the spider, 'is Charlotte.' 'Charlotte what?' asked Wilbur eagerly."

"You come back next week," Tabor ordered.

Shannon and Tabor were outside in the shadows of Shenandoah Avenue. "I plan to, Tabor," she said.

"You call me first. I let you know when to come." Tabor leaned against Shannon's car door so she couldn't open it.

"I'll come about the same time, I think."

"You call me first, hear. I let you know if it's awright to come then. You can't come here less I meet you. Mamma

27

say that too." He pulled his hair with his comb and stared hard into her eyes. "You not safe here by yourself and don't start thinking you are. You come because we say you can."

"Well, Tabor..." Shannon's voice sharpened.

"Same time be awright though, I think." He opened the car door. Shannon didn't say anything. " 'Bout this same time, I'd say," he repeated. "I watch for you, hear."

It was the fourth tutoring session when the children first heard their mother read. Corene and Shannon were working at the kitchen table where they always worked, and the children were watching television in the living room. About midway through the lesson Shannon heard a rustling sound at the edge of the room. When she looked up, she didn't see anything at first, but then she spotted the top of a head and two sets of fingers behind the wide back of the arm chair. Corry and Tabor peeked out then quickly ducked into hiding. Shannon tried to wave them away, but they wouldn't look at her. They crouched low in the chair and listened to their mother.

" 'If I can fool a bug,' thought Charlotte, 'I can surely fool a man. People are not as smart as bugs.' " Corene plodded through the sentences punctuating every other word. " 'There's a regular con...con...con-spiracy...' " Shannon winced as the children listened to their mother read. She hoped they couldn't hear from where they sat, but when Corry and Tabor peered from around the chair a second time, she knew that they had heard. Corry's lips pushed out in a pout, and her eyes pleaded with her mother to read different words. Tabor's jaw set; his face was angry and allowed no room for reason.

After Shannon finished the lesson that evening, Tabor followed her to her car. "Why Ma reading that book?" he demanded.

"That's the one she chose," Shannon answered carefully.

"She can't finish high school reading that."

"It will take longer," Shannon said. "She's forgotten some things."

28

Tabor started to pace beside the car. "Oh man!" he muttered. "How much they paying you to teach Ma?"

"Nobody's paying me. I want to teach her."

"We don't need your charity," Tabor announced. He thrust his hand into his pocket. "I'll pay you."

"I don't want your money, Tabor."

"I'll pay what you want then you pass her on that test." Tabor pulled out a ten-dollar bill. "I work; I got money."

"I don't have anything to do with that test," Shannon said. "The state gives the test."

"The state? Ah man!" He hit his hand on top of the car. "What they know? They don know Ma's smart. They fail her. I know even before she try, they goin fail her. She readin about sheep and pigs and bugs. They ain't going pass that." He reached into his pocket and pulled out another five-dollar bill; it was the last of his money. "You could get a copy of the test and teach her the answers. She get a good job then."

"Your mother wouldn't want me to do that," Shannon tried.

"Shit!" he declared. "She don have to know."

"Tabor, I can't. If I wanted to, I couldn't get that test."

Tabor grew still. Shannon tried to see what he was thinking, but instead she saw him disappear behind a wall in himself. He shoved the money into his pocket. "You don understand," he said. "You don understand nothing." He turned from her. Then looking back over his shoulder, he issued his final indictment: "You never gwonna understand either." And he stalked away.

Tabor and Corry wouldn't speak to Shannon when she came to tutor the next week. They sat sullenly in the livingroom, and Shannon spent the whole time with Corene, who continued to treat her like a stranger in her home. The following week they ignored her as well and the week after that.

Shannon had hoped to be closer to this family by now. She had come to Baltimore after college graduation to learn about a world that wasn't her own. She'd left Raleigh, North Carolina where life, it seemed to her, was swallowed up like

29

the sticks she used to throw into mud holes as a child. The mud simply closed around what was offered it and remained unchanged. She had come to Baltimore, a city where she knew no one, to live unadorned, stripped to some essential she hadn't yet discovered. She lived in a single room in a run-down boarding house, worked at an inner city library and tried by proximity to absorb the otherness of other people's lives.

Besides the Roberts, however, she had met few people. She spent her days patching library books and watching the round, unsmiling clock on the library wall. At lunch hour she walked the streets; she listened to the voices of "Secret Storm" and "Guiding Light" droning out the windows. At night as she returned to her room, the boredom she'd felt all day grew into a tight, unfocused anxiety. The faces she passed on the street seemed suspicious of her living in this part of the city. When she smiled at them, they wouldn't accept her smile, and so she had begun to hold her own face expressionless: her jaw set and her eyes blank. She had tied her possibilities to the Roberts, and now the distance between them threatened a larger loneliness in herself.

In the fourth week after Tabor and Corry had imposed their silence, Shannon took the test. She got it through the library where she worked. She told herself she would only use it as a study aid. She told Tabor he mustn't say a word to his mother. She also told him she might lose her job for borrowing the test. She exaggerated the risk to herself, but she wanted Tabor to appreciate what she'd done.

Tabor answered, "Well, that your problem, isn't it?"

Tabor had taken to battling Corene whenever Shannon was around, and the night she told him she had the test, he escalated the battle. He wanted to go to a friend's house, and his mother had told him he couldn't.

"Shit, I can leave if I want," he declared. "Who you think I am anyway? Bumper or some kid? Shit!"

"You ain't goin an that's all the more I want t' hear," Corene snapped. "I'm tutoring tonight, an you ain't done the dishes like you suppose; you ain't cleaned; you jes thinkin only about yourself all the time."

"Howcome I got t' do everything? I'm fifteen next month; that ain't no kid. Howcome Corry don't have t' do them dishes?"

"Corry cooked dinner," Corene said calmly. Corry smiled up at Tabor.

"You jes shut up!" he snapped at his sister. "You think you so smart ass, that shit-grin all over your face. Jes you wait till you want something..." Tabor marched into his and Bumper's room and slammed the door.

Corry and Shannon and Corene sat at the table in silence. Inside Tabor's room a shoe hit against the wall. From the corner of the kitchen Bumper suddenly crashed one of his cars into the sink. He looked up at his mother daring her to stop him. Karoom Bang! Another truck hit head on into the wall.

Tabor stuck his head out. "You jes reading kids books anyway, Ma!" He hurled his final charge. "You ain't even know how to read!" Then he slammed the door, and the door frame shook around it.

Corry's eyes darted to her mother then quickly looked away. Corene sat in her blue cornflowered housedress staring at the books in the bag. Shannon fingered a plastic daisy in the jelly jar in the middle of the table. Both she and Corry waited, watching for some sign of Tabor's blow. Finally Corene reached for the box of starch beside her, and dumping it into the palm of her hand, she began to lick the powder.

Corry shoved up from the table. She marched over to the sink and dug her hands into the dishes.

"You leave them dishes alone," Corene ordered. "Them's Tabor's, and he's going to do them."

"But, Ma..." Corry protested.

"I mean it."

"I can wash them..." she pleaded, but Corene wouldn't listen. Corry dropped the plate and shut off the water. She stalked out of the kitchen into the living room where she jerked on the tv and dragged a tattered chair in front of the screen. Bumper glanced quickly at his mother then grabbed his trucks and scurried after Corry.

At the table Shannon waited for Corene to speak. Corene sucked on her starch and began rearranging the flowers in the jar. "I got to git Tabor some new shoes," she said. "That boy kill a pair of sneakers like he had vengeance on them." Shannon nodded. "He's gettin so big. Sometimes I think he's bigger n he is then I see he's still a chile...just a chile." Corene spoke as though she were talking to herself, and she looked off somewhere Shannon couldn't follow. "It's hard for him growing up. He don think I know, but I know." She smoothed down the table cloth with the palm of her hand.

"Tabor's not the one what worries me though," she went on. "It's Bumper. Tabor, he lets everything out, and it's over; he yells and he curses and he'll stay in his room half the night, but then it's over. Corry, she's more that way too, like Tabor, only she don usually git real mad; she likely as not to start laughing at herself. But Bumper he keeps it all inside hisself...like his daddy..." She sipped the water. "He don know it, but he jes like his daddy."

Shannon didn't answer. Corene had never talked to her this way before. Shannon wasn't sure if she were talking to her or setting out some order for herself. Finally Shannon ventured, "Bumper's lucky to have a brother and sister. I don't have much family."

Corene glanced up as if surprised to hear her speak. "They do treat him nice," she agreed. She pulled out her glasses from her housedress. "Most folks call me Rennie," she said. "You call me that too if you like."

"Yes," Shannon said. "I'd like that."

Rennie nodded. She wiped the glasses with the hem of her dress; then putting them on, she began to read.

"I'm sorry, Ma," Tabor pushed out of his room, sending his words before him like an advance guard. He sulked over to the refrigerator and took out an apple. He lingered in the door daring his mother to speak to him.

"'Wilbur never forgot Charlotte,'" Rennie read out. "'Although he loved her children and grandchildren dearly, none of the new spiders ever quite took her place in his heart ...It is not often that someone comes along who is a true friend and a good writer. Charlotte was both.'" Tabor listened. Rennie shut the book. "That was a good book," she said, speaking to Shannon but watching her son, "...a good book."

Tabor shut the refrigerator door. He glanced at his mother, and without a word, he withdrew to the living room.

"I think he understands," Shannon said.

Rennie shook her head. "He don understand. But he'll let it be."

From the living room Corry suddenly shouted. "You leave me 'lone. We was doin just fine till you come in here spoiling things. You leave that tv alone."

"Aw Miss Smart Ass, you ain't own the world," Tabor answered.

"Well, you ain't own nothin!" she snapped. "You ruinin everything tonight." Her voice suddenly lowered. Her face filled with anger, and her words fired out like close range, high-speed bullets, "We-promise-not-to-tell-Ma-we-knew-an-you-got-to-tell-her-jes-cause-you-get-mad-You-nothin-Tabor-Roberts-you-nothin!"

Tabor stared at Corry wide-eyed; he tried to comprehend what he'd done. "Shit!..." he stammered finally. "Shit!" He grabbed his coat and started for the door, but then he spun around. "So I'm nothin, huh?" he asked. "I tell you how nothin I am. I got the tutor t' steal that test for us. I got her to steal that test so Ma could pass. Thas how nothin I am!" And he bolted into the night.

At the kitchen table Shannon didn't move. She stared at the workbooks in front of her. She could feel Rennie watching her. She began to gather the books.

"You steal that test?" Rennie asked.

Shannon dropped her notebook then a workbook into her bag. "I borrowed it," she said without looking up, "...at the library where I work."

"Why you do that?"

"I wanted to check some things." She dropped *Charlotte's Web* into the bag. "I wanted to make sure you were learning the right things."

"You think I got to cheat to pass a test?"

"No. I... It's just that sometimes those tests aren't fair."

"What you mean not fair?"

"I mean to your background."

"What background you talkin about?"

Shannon glanced up; her expression pleaded with Rennie. "They're not always fair," she insisted.

Rennie sucked on her starch and sipped water from the jelly jar. "Because I'm colored you mean." Shannon didn't answer. "I lived my whole life with not fair," Rennie said, "but I don recollect I ast you to steal me no test, and I ain't ast you to get my childrens in stealing tests." Rennie rose from the table and went over to the sink. "You still a child yourself, I see," she said. "It makes me wonder when they send *you* to teach *me*." And she dug her hands into the cold, greasy water, and she began to wash the dishes.

Baltimore, 1968

Shannon lived in Baltimore alone. She lived in a rooming house on a wide treeless street between a funeral parlor and a boarded-up building. The house was an aging Victorian brownstone among the flattop row houses on the block, its lattice work chipped away, its ceilings bowed as if repentant over lost dignity. On the front windows padlocks barred intruders, and at the front desk a two hundred-pound matron named Ruby sat watching over the house inside.

Outside people moved past day and night: jive-walking, high-stepping, heel-clicking men with radios to their ears and cocksure hats tilted over one eye; housekeeping women running, plodding to catch the Number 8 bus to Towson, the 14 to Glen Burnie; Jewish grannies, grey-haired, grey-faced meeting at Hymie's deli where pigs' feet and salami sold side by side.

Across the street from Ruby's was the Green Mount Cemetery, one of Baltimore's old landmarks filled with the famous and the dead. It was closed off from the streets by a high stone wall which rose out of the rubble of the city like a fortress from the past and was crowned with jutting rocks and draped with ivy and honeysuckle, morning glories and lilacs.

On one of the early, hot evenings of September, Shannon stopped by this wall. The cemetery was the only green area in this part of the city, and she wanted inside to lie under a tree. The evening was warm and close, and she didn't want

35

to go back to Ruby's yet. Honeysuckle filled the early night air, and as she stood staring at the grass and the flowers on the other side, her thoughts drifted back for a moment to the ripe green smells of home: the mint, the baby onions, the wisteria hanging over the garage. She had come here from Raleigh, North Carolina where her father lived in a sprawling house in an all-white enclave of the city. She had come after college graduation to break with her past and create herself from that which she was not. She had also come "to help" though who or how she would help she wasn't sure, and she wouldn't have argued that it was also herself she was helping for she wanted to close the distance between who she was and who she might become, between the experience handed her and experience she must seek for herself.

Shannon tried the gate to the cemetery again, but it held fast. Finally turning from the graveyard, she faced the street. At the end of the block the sun was sinking behind the Esso station. As she darted over the avenue against the light, a horn honked.

At Ruby's she mounted the steps slowly. From the corner of the stoop a small, wide-eyed woman watched her. "They don ever open that gate, Sharry," she said. The woman stared out over the graveyard. "I been here seven years, and they ain't never opened that gate yet. They just got one gate to get in, one to get out. That's a white folks graveyard."

From the porch Shannon glanced back across the street. She could see over the wall now; the hills, the trees, the weeping marble ladies.

"Yes, I been here seven years, and they ain't never opened that gate yet." The woman picked her teeth with a match and waited for Shannon to answer.

"It's nice in there."

"Yeah, it nice; it real nice," the woman said. "Grass, flowers, markers on every grave. When I go, I'm going to a place like that." She spit out the splinters of the match she was chewing. "Course I'm only twenty-six years old; I ain't goin yet. I been living here since I was nineteen. How old you? Bout twenty I'd say."

"I'm twenty-one," Shannon answered. She stood uneasily in front of the woman.

"What I figured. I always been good measuring ages; I don know why. Some things 'bout a person I can see right off; I can see right inside some people." She considered Shannon. "Like I know you a little afraid of me. See, I can tell. You don't know what to make of me. Well, that's okay. Lots of people feels that way. But see, I'm twenty-six years old, and I can do what I want. My mother can't even tell me what to do no more...no one can."

The woman stuck out her chin then broke out laughing at herself. She reached up and grabbed Shannon's hand to pull her down. Her own hands were rough and coarse like a man's, and her face, puffy, moon-shaped, was not soft. There was a frantic look about her, in the small button eyes that darted from person to person on the street, in the quick, relentless way she held to Shannon's hand. Her two front teeth were missing, and her cheeks were swollen and bruised. On this hot night she wore slacks and a long-sleeved shirt covering her small body, and around her neck and hands Shannon could see the darker, shiny skin of scars. The violence on this woman's body startled her.

"Sit down," the woman insisted. "I'll talk to you if I want. See, I don care what peoples say about me, Sharry." She glanced at the neighbors watching on the other stoops.

"My name's Shannon," Shannon said.

"That's right, honey, I know. And my name's Emmeline. Now tell me, you staying here long, Sharry? I'll be glad to have some nice company for a change."

"I don't know really...I'm not sure yet." Shannon dropped her notebook and sat down on the stoop.

"What make you sure? When you think you know? When I came here, I didn't know I'd be staying this long either. I've been here seven years now. But see, I got married; that's why I stay on. You not married yet, are you? No, I see you not." She glanced at Shannon's ringless hand. "You haven't met Rud yet; he's my husband." She lowered her eyes, and for a moment she was quiet; then softly she added, "Rud don't like white much." Shannon looked over at her, and Emmeline flashed a smile and groped for Shannon's hand. "I don't mean nothing personal by saying that, you understand; it's just the way he is. He always been that way."

Shannon nodded. She was still staring at the damage on this woman's body. "I understand." She offered a smile, but Emmeline looked at her suspiciously now.

"How you understand? You don understand." She took back her hand. "Why you always carrying that notebook around? What you do? You in school? Look like you always got something to write down in that notebook." Emmeline stared at the three-ring binder between them.

"I write for myself," Shannon explained. "It's just something I do."

Emmeline watched her with small, wary eyes. "You ever write poems?" she asked. She touched the notebook. "I write poems myself. I hides them away." She paused. "Rud gets mad when he sees me writing them. He thinks it's crazy." She considered Shannon, and carefully she added, "I show you my poems someday if you like."

"Yes, I'd like that."

Emmeline nodded; then she looked out on the street as though satisfied that she had set this white girl at ease.

Shannon and Emmeline sat on the stoop in silence for a while. At the end of the block the streetlights blinked on, and the two women watched the evening crowd begin to gather at Ned's Bar on the corner.

All of a sudden Emmeline broke into a high, forced laugh. "You know what I was just thinking?" she said. "Now that we friends, I bet you go over to Ned's and get me a beer, wouldn't you?" She put her hand on Shannon's knee, and her dry, rasping voice honeyed. "I'd go myself, you understand, but Rud he told Ned he ain't to sell me no more to drink." Emmeline reached into her pocket and took out a dime. She placed it in Shannon's hand. "I only got ten cent, but it cost you more, I pay you back. Get yourself one too. Hot night like this a body needs something."

Shannon hesitated, but Emmeline pushed the dime into her hand and urged her to go. Finally Shannon stood up; then taking the money, she started over to Ned's.

Ned's Bar was a one-room cellar just below street level. In the evenings it filled with people, and tonight there were so many people Shannon could barely see the bar. The air was thick with smoke, and the room smelled of whiskey and damp rotting wood. Shannon stood in the doorway for a moment; then she started to maneuver her way across the room. As she went, a man watched her from the bar. He was a tall, lean white man with shaggy brown hair and a smile that played insolently at the edges of his mouth. When Shannon spotted him, he nodded, but she turned away. At the counter she ordered a beer and a coke then stood waiting for her order. Other men stared at her now, and she straightened her body and tried to look as though she had a purpose there. Finally the bartender slid her drinks down to her, and as she turned to take them, she saw the man still watching. She dropped her money on the counter; then gathering up the drinks, she went quickly out the door.

Back at Ruby's, Emmeline was waving and chatting to whomever passed by, and Shannon dropped down onto the step beside her. As she popped open her can, the man from the bar walked up.

"So she got *you* to buy for her tonight," he said. He wore faded cutoffs, a T-shirt, and sandals, and he spoke in a wry, quiet voice.

Emmeline cast him a warning glance. "You two know each other?" she asked.

"I saw her in Ned's buying your beer."

Emmeline watched him. "Well, this here's Sharry," she said cautiously. "Sharry, this Wainwright. Sharry's a nice girl, Wainwright," Emmeline started defending. "She's a very nice girl living here for a time."

"I can see she's a nice girl, can't I? Is it all right if I talk to her or you got her staked out for Rud?"

Emmeline drew herself up, and her lips started fighting to get words out, "Don make no fun of me, Wainwright," she warned.

"I ain't makin fun of you, Em. Who says I'm makin fun of you?"

"I don like that name either. My name's Emmeline. I ain't no Em. My name's Emmeline."

Wainwright glanced over at Shannon. "She's a bit tetched," he said. Shannon frowned.

"I ain't tetched. You just go to the debil. You never been any good, never will be any good. You just go to the debil; he'll wax your hide in hell!" Emmeline wrapped her arms around herself and leaned up against the wall, and her body shrank into the corner.

Shannon arranged her face to give this man a disapproving look; her brow narrowed, and her mouth grew tight; but an interest flickered in her eyes, and Wainwright nodded to the interest. "Well, if you ladies will excuse me," he said. "I'll be retiring for the night." And he turned and went into Ruby's without looking back.

Shannon glanced over at Emmeline and waited for her to speak. Emmeline sipped on her beer and stared out over the graveyard. "I'm twenty-six years old," she said, "and I can do what I want." She looked down at her hands then folded them into fists, hiding the burned fingers. "Some people say I'm crazy. I know they say it, but I ain't. It hurts my soul to hear them say it, but I ain't crazy. I'm twenty-six years old, and I can do what I want..."

Shannon and Emmeline stayed out on the steps till past midnight. The neighbors around them deserted the stoops one by one, picking up their beer cans and cards and papers, but Shannon and Emmeline postponed going in as long as possible. Outside the night was cool, and people still moved about them. Finally Shannon gathered her books and rose from the steps, and Emmeline followed.

As Shannon turned towards her room on the second floor, Emmeline grabbed her hand. "You got to go in now?"

she asked.

Shannon nodded. "I work tomorrow."

"Oh..." Emmeline said. Her eyes darted up and down the hall. "That's where Wainwright lives." She pointed to the light under 2D. "He's a photographer; he got himself a darkroom in there. Sometimes I wished I lived on the second floor." She looked about for another reason to stay.

"Good night," Shannon insisted.

"Oh, yeah..." Emmeline said. And finally she turned from Shannon and walked towards the staircase. Slowly she mounted the narrow steps, holding tight to the banister, and she forced her way to the third floor.

Inside her room, Shannon dumped her books on the bed and fumbled in the dark for the small bedside light. She opened a window to flush out the sick sweet smell of dead air and stale sheets, a window she would close and lock before she went to bed. She had lived in this room over a month, but it was as alien to her now as the day she'd moved in. In one corner a cot leaned against the wall; beside it was a wing chair, grease-spotted with the cushion missing, then a desk, a table, a dresser. In the far corner of the room stood a toilet, a sink, a towel rack hung with threadbare towels, and off the room, hidden behind a food-stained curtain, was a small icebox and a two-burner hotplate.

The room looked out over an alley. One of the window shades was missing, and the window opened her room up to the outside like a great dark eye of night. Shannon was afraid of that window. She'd tried hanging newspaper over it, but the paper fell down in the middle of the night with a rustle that sent her bolting upright in bed. While those outside could see in, she could never see out. She would turn off the light and creep to the edge of the window to see if anyone were looking, but all she could see was the dark. Shannon had argued with Ruby to fix the shade so many times that Ruby now neglected it on principle, and Shannon was forced to live in the shadows of her room. She never turned on the overhead light; she read, worked, ate by the tiny bedside lamp. She had yet to undress at night for she felt too vulnerable in only the thin nylon of her nightgown so she slept in her clothes on top of the bed in a room with locked windows, and she slept a stuffy and uneasy sleep.

Shannon had thought by now she would fit in better here, but until tonight she had met no one at Ruby's. She had tried introducing herself to a few of her neighbors, but they didn't seem interested in knowing her. They simply nodded then disappeared into their rooms. She spent most of her evenings alone in her room reading and writing and listening to the voices through the walls. She would hear her neighbor Mrs. Epstein playing her radio all night. "What time is it, Harry?" Mrs. Epstein would whisper. "What time is it?" Shannon would then hear sweeping — she thought it was sweeping — a dry, scraping sound of straw over the floor. She heard this sound constantly, this sweeping, this cleaning out. "Harry, hold my hand," Mrs. Epstein would call, but no voice ever answered back.

Shannon set her books on the floor now and turned out the lamp. She closed the window, and lying down on the cot, she watched the lights from the other buildings send shadows over her walls. The fear which seeped into her each night began to creep over her now. She hadn't counted on this fear. She wondered if everyone who lived here was afraid. She was ashamed and annoyed that she couldn't find her ease in this place. She looked up through the darkness. Above her plaster hung water-stained and flaking from the ceiling, damp ceiling, dried then wet then dried again, musty lonesome smell of a room rented then abandoned, of servants' quarters beside the garage, of old furniture and old servants sharing the same quarters. She shut her eyes, and as she lay on this strange bed, in a strange room, she felt she was living somewhere out of time.

A scream startled Shannon awake. She wasn't sure if the scream came from outside or from her dreams. She lay in the dark listening. Nothing. The noises of the building had quieted to an early morning hush, and only the drone of Elsie Epstein's radio next door murmured in the silence. Shannon turned on the light. She sat barely breathing, looking about for the sound of the scream. Slowly she got up and began to walk around, first in her room, then finally out into the hallway. The scream had frightened her, but it was the quiet after the scream which lingered inside.

She longed to talk with someone. At the end of the hall she saw a light under Wainwright's door. She thought of going to talk with him, but there had been something about him which had disarmed her. He was older than she though she couldn't tell how much older. He had a desultory way about him which fit into this neighborhood; yet there was something which did not fit in. He had looked at her as though he saw her in her own territory, a place they both knew while at the same time he reduced her to the ground where she now stood. His look had both offended and attracted her. She stared down the hall into the silence. Gathering her courage, she finally moved slowly towards the light.

At Wainwright's door Shannon knocked, a shy tentative rap. "It's Shannon," she whispered, "from across the hall." No one answered. She knocked again. She started to turn away when the door opened, and Wainwright peered into the hall. Barefooted, bare-chested, he still wore cutoff jeans. He stood unmoving as though he didn't see her.

"I'm sorry..." she said. "You were sleeping." She started to leave.

"No," he answered. He stared at her waiting to hear why she'd come.

"I heard a scream," she explained. "I saw your light. Am I bothering you?"

"No." But still he didn't invite her in.

She shifted on her feet. "I thought you might know what happened." For a moment he didn't answer. Again she started to turn, but this time he moved out of the doorway and motioned her inside. She hesitated now, but then straightening her shoulders, she passed into the room.

Wainwright's room was filled with photographs. Giant pictures covered the walls: bits of steel on a deserted playground, pipes funneling one into another — hole inside hole towards a never-ending point — the demolition arm of a crane crashing into an old tenement. Shannon felt as though she'd entered someone's imagination turned inside out then tacked up on the walls.

"I don't usually let people in my room," Wainwright said.

"Oh?" She cleared her throat. Her eyes skipped around the walls. "Did you take these?" Wainwright nodded and moved over to his desk where he sat down and returned to his work. He bent over a stack of photographs and began measuring them with a ruler.

"I am bothering you," she said. "I'll go."

"No." He spoke flatly without turning around, and yet his voice told her he wanted her to stay. He continued working with his back to her. The tight, hard muscles in his shoulders flexed as he sorted through the pictures. His skin was pale and looked as though it never saw sunlight.

Shannon began to look about the room. Clothes were slumped on the floor; sheets brownish yellow lay crumpled at the end of the bed; photography magazines were strewn on tables, under chairs, and there were cigarette butts everywhere. Only his work corner was ordered: paper, pictures, chemicals all stacked in their proper niches. Shannon stepped over the clothes to the walls, and she began to study the photographs. She stood in front of them as though she were in a museum. She leaned close, stepped back, considered them from different angles. She concentrated on her form more than on the pictures for she wanted to look independent and occupied. At one picture she paused. In it empty army boots stood circling a lone grave. She glanced at other pictures on the walls, and all at once she realized there were no people in these pictures; there was only the implication of people, somewhere beyond the graveyard, watching just out of sight of the demolished homes.

She stepped over to the next wall when Wainwright turned. "Please...sit down." His words were more order than invitation, and he moved between her and the wall. "Please."

"I can only stay a few minutes," she insisted. "I heard a scream..."

"So you said."

"I saw your light..."

Wainwright sat on the bed; then he lay back on the pillow and cupped his hands behind his head. He lay stretched before her in only his shorts. She peered at him from under her bangs. He was handsome in a dark and off-handed way. His face was hidden behind a beard. His jaw was narrow; his nose, sharp, and his eyes gazed out from a great arched forehead like two cool agate marbles. The lines around his eyes and mouth made him look older than the thirty years she guessed him to be. "Didn't you hear it?" she asked. She crossed her legs and wished her skirt weren't so short.

"I hear people screaming all night." He focused on the arc of her calves, the narrow curve of legs slightly thin.

"I couldn't get back to sleep; I thought you might know where it came from." She kept her legs perfectly still.

"You're not safe chasing screams," Wainwright said. His eyes held her whole body frozen before him. Her arms and legs were slender and stretched out like long limbs attached to a stubby trunk. She wore no makeup, and her hair cupped loosely below her ears. "What are you doing at Ruby's anyway?" he asked.

Shannon pulled her hands out from under her now as if needing them for her defense. "I work around here..." she said, "...at a new library over by Gay Street. It's an old warehouse actually that we're fixing up into a library. We take old books from the other libraries and try to make them look new..." She heard her words rattling out, and she stopped. For a moment she didn't say anything; then looking at Wainwright, she asked, "What do you do?" She glanced at the darkroom constructed out of plywood around the sink. "I mean I see you're a photographer, but is that what you do professionally?"

"Professionally?" Wainwright asked.

"I mean for a living. Do you take pictures for a living?"

"Do I make money taking pictures...is that what you mean?"

"Yes, I guess it is."

"No, I don't make any money."

"Oh..." She paused. "Well, you take interesting pictures."

Wainwright stared, attentive, skeptical. "Why are they interesting?"

She looked at him to see if he really wanted to know; then she stood and moved back to the walls. Her lips drew together as she stared at the photographs. There was a seriousness about her, behind the innocence of her large eyes and the awkwardness of her body frozen under his stare. There was a purpose held tight within.

"They're ordered..." she said finally. "They're ordered and geometric, and yet they're about disorder. You catch things just before they fall apart." She looked over at him smiling, pleased with her analysis.

Wainwright reached for a cigarette on the nightstand. "Why did you come to my room tonight?" he asked.

"I told you; I heard a scream. I was afraid. I don't know anyone here."

"What do you want to prove living here?"

"Nothing."

Wainwright lit his cigarette.

"Why do you live here?" she asked.

"People leave me alone here."

"Well, I want to meet new people."

Wainwright laughed suddenly, a short, surprised laugh. "You think this is a sorority house?"

Shannon stiffened her shoulders. "No."

"Good. Because Ruby's no dorm mother to take care of you."

Shannon didn't answer. She grew still. She stared out the window. She watched a man weaving down the street. Without looking around, said said, "Don't try to tell me why

I'm here." The stillness in her voice made Wainwright stare. She stood by the window with odd ends of her hair frayed against the light. Her skirt hung wrinkled over her round hips; her white blouse was rumpled and stained with spots of purple juice. Finally she turned around, and her tone was more conciliatory. "I wonder if you'd do me a favor?" she asked.

Wainwright opened his hands, gesturing for her to go on.

"Through the library, I'm tutoring this black family," she said. "Would you take their picture?" She sat back down on the chair.

"I don't do that kind of photography."

"The mother asked me a while ago if I had a camera. She wants a picture for their grandmother. You might enjoy meeting them." A flush rose on her pale skin; she was self-conscious at sounding naive, but she was trying to offer some bridge to this man. "They don't want anything fancy," she added. She crossed her legs. On her feet she wore heavy Weejun loafers of her college days. "I'd do it myself, but I didn't bring a camera."

Wainwright's eyes traced the beginning curve of her thigh under her skirt. He was about to say he'd take the picture when she caught his gaze and flicked down her hem. She smiled at him then as if her gesture were only a friendly rebuke, but Wainwright said instead, "You'll have to help the coloreds on your own." He snubbed his cigarette on the nightstand and struck a match to light another one.

Shannon frowned. She thought he was making a bad joke, but his eyes were steady upon her. She stood and moved towards the door. "I guess I'd better go." Wainwright rose from the bed and stepped in front of her. "I really have to go," Shannon insisted. She reached for the doorknob, but Wainwright took her arm. "Please..." Her face tightened. "You're hurting me." She stood facing him, and her eyes were wide and rebellious now.

He stared, his eyes judging hers. "I am not hurting you," he said. Then he squeezed her arm and tossed it aside. He moved back over to his desk and looked down at his photographs.

Shannon stood behind him. Suddenly she wanted to hurt him; she didn't know why, but she wanted to hurt. "Why aren't there any people in your pictures?" she asked.

"What?"

"I just wondered why there were no people in your pictures."

Wainwright turned around. He glanced at her, then at the walls. He stared at the photographs one by one — the picture of the playground, the photo of the boots in the graveyard. He dropped his cigarette to the floor and crushed it. His hair fell over his forehead; he looked tired. Shannon saw the deep creases around the edges of his eyes, and as suddenly as she'd wanted to hurt, she wanted to take the hurt away.

"I like your pictures. I didn't mean..." she tried, but he wasn't listening.

Instead he said, "Get out..." His voice was a dead calm. "Just get out."

Shannon didn't see Wainwright again for almost a month. The first few days she was relieved to avoid him; he was too self-absorbed, too indifferent to people, she told herself. But when she didn't see him for two weeks, she began to look for him among the faces on the street and among the patrons passing in and out of Ned's. He was the only man she had met here who offered any interest or possibility though she hadn't admitted to herself the possibilities. But when she came inside in the evenings, she would move past his room pausing in the light that crept from under his door. In the mornings when she left for work, she would see this same light, a yellow strip washed in the grey dawn of the hallway. She never heard a sound from his room. After a while she began to wonder if he still lived there, but on Mondays when clean towels were hung on the doorknobs, his disappeared, and she knew someone was inside.

On a Saturday afternoon in early October, Wainwright emerged.

All week a suffocating haze had hung onto the city in a last hold of summer. Finally it had rained hard and long during the night and into the morning. When the sun at last broke through and the air dawned cool and crisp around three in the afternoon, Shannon joined Emmeline outside on the stoop. Emmeline was sitting on the bottom step, crouched over, playing tag with a small brown and white puppy. The puppy hid beneath the bottom step then every few minutes poked its head out and came bounding into the sunshine. When it pounced in front of Emmeline, she would stomp her foot at it, and the puppy would scurry back to cover. As they played this game, Emmeline shrieked in a high-pitched laugh.

"You a smart debil, Pup!" she declared. "Smart as dog I ever seen." She stomped again. "There!" she cried, and the puppy jumped back. Stomp! "There!" And the puppy dodged again, its stubby tail pumping fast with excitement. "Ain't he smart!" Emmeline declared as Shannon moved down beside her. "Didn't I tell you he was smart?"

Shannon reached out to pet the dog, and the puppy darted back.

"See! He don let no one touch him either," Emmeline boasted. "I taught him that too. I found him, and he's mine." She bent down and lifted the puppy onto the steps. "But I teach him to like you." She held the dog towards Shannon. "I call him Pup. He already know how to stay outta people's way so he don get stept on. Smarter n most people I know."

Shannon reached out, and this time pet the dog's floppy ears. "You keeping him upstairs?" she asked.

Emmeline set the puppy in her lap. "Not jes yet," she said evasively. She reached into her pocket and pulled out of handful of popcorn and fed it to the puppy. "Rud don't like dogs much. I'm keeping Pup here under the house for a while." She glanced at Shannon. "Just till it get cold, you understand. Rud, he afraid of dogs, and he get mean to them. He got bit once," she explained quickly. "He think all dogs mean and pee all over everything." She drew her matted black sweater around the puppy. "Rud don't like anything he don't understand."

Shannon started to answer when the front door swung open, and there standing in the sunlight, squinting up at the sky, was Wainwright. He wore a frayed blue sweater without a shirt and jeans bleached white at the knee. Instead of his sandals, he had on heavy brown work boots, and over his arm he carried a camera. Shannon stared at him for a moment trying to recognize him. His face was more worn than she remembered. As he stood there, he dragged on a cigarette. He cupped the cigarette inward towards his palm, and he cupped the palm towards himself, and he seemed as hidden and contained as that cigarette which was slowly burning itself to ashes.

"Wel-l-l," Emmeline greeted. "So you out in the worl' again? To what do we owe this honor?"

"I saw *you* out here, Em," he said. He moved down onto the step next to Shannon.

Emmeline watched him cautiously. "You remember Sharry?" she asked.

"Sharry, the librarian, isn't it?"

"Shannon," Shannon said.

"Yes, Shannon. You had any more bad dreams lately, Shannon?" His tone was patronizing, and she frowned. "I haven't seen you lately."

"All the better for her I'd say," Emmeline sallied.

Wainwright sat down on the step. He reached over to pet the puppy. His face moved within inches of Shannon's, but Shannon didn't move.

Emmeline jerked the puppy away. "You be careful," she warned.

"I'm not going to hurt your dog. You know I take care of innocent creatures."

"I know what kind care you take," Emmeline answered.

Wainwright patted the puppy's rump. "Now, Em, you don't want to give Shannon here the wrong impression, do you?"

Emmeline laughed. "This girls got brains, Wainwright. She already got herself an impression."

Wainwright looked over at Shannon, who kept her eyes on the dog. "You know I think you're right," he said. Shannon didn't answer. She stroked the puppy's head, her fingers coddling the soft crown between his ears. She was intensely aware of this man's presence beside her, but she tried not to show any interest. Wainwright smiled for he saw what she would not recognize. Finally he turned to Emmeline. "Rud know you got this dog?"

Emmeline drew the dog to her. "Never you mind what Rud know."

"You know what he'll do if he catches you."

"Rud at work," Emmeline defended.

"Well, it's your ass." Wainwright started adjusting the camera, aiming it first at the street then towards Emmeline. "Just don't come crying to me when Rud beats it off."

"Don't you worry none; I ain't crying to you." Emmeline began buttoning her sweater around the puppy. She stuffed the puppy's head inside and tried to hide the dog. "An don't you take no pictures of me, Wainwright. Don't you do it! You put that camera away." She bent her head down into her lap, and the puppy yelped. "Hush up now," she declared. "Hush up, Pup." But the puppy squirmed to get air, and suddenly Emmeline jumped to her feet dropping the dog to the pavement. "Shit!" she cried. "That Pup bit me!" Her eyes darted to Wainwright. "He bit me," she repeated.

Shannon reached out for the dog and took it in her arms. She glanced quickly at Wainwright then at Emmeline. She didn't understand why Wainwright was tormenting her. She began stroking the puppy's head and talking to it. She held the dog out to Emmeline. "It's all right. He couldn't breathe; he got afraid."

Emmeline stared at the puppy. "He afraid?" she asked. Shannon nodded, and Emmeline reached out and touched the dog's head cautiously. "He jes afraid." She began petting the dog. "You don got to be afraid, Pup."

"That's why Rud won't let you have pets," Wainwright said. "He's afraid you'll kill them."

"Rud scared a dogs. That's why." She hugged the puppy. "He don like dogs."

Wainwright moved down onto the sidewalk. "Well, you do what you want." He started walking away; then he glanced back. "I'm going to shoot some pictures," he said to Shannon, and almost as an afterthought, he added, "You want to come?"

Shannon looked over at Emmeline. She was cradling the puppy now like a baby and singing to it; she didn't notice Shannon anymore. "A'ready know how to stay outta people's way," she muttered. "Smartest pup I ever seen."

Shannon hesitated; then slowly she rose. Wainwright didn't wait for her, but she noticed that he slowed his pace until she caught up. He didn't attempt a conversation and so neither did she. She glanced at him out of the corner of her eye. His face was hidden behind his beard, but she could see his small clear eyes darting from person to person on the street. He seemed to take each one in with a look which both saw them and gazed beyond them.

Emmeline had told her what little she knew about Wainwright, that he'd come to Ruby's two years ago, arrived late one night with only a suitcase, a camera, and a folder under his arm, that he rarely came out of his room those first months. Even now he went into his room for weeks sometimes, Emmeline said. When he did come out, he spent his time at bars and in the crowds at Ned's. "Seem like all he do is work on those pictures day and night though I never once seen him take a picture," Emmeline had told her. "You know he been to college, some fancy college, but he don't act like no college boy. He act like a man lost hisself a long time ago."

What she didn't know about Wainwright interested Shannon as much as what she did. She tried to think of something to say now. "Where are you going?" she asked finally.

He pointed to the cemetery wall that rose beside them.

"I've never been in there."

He didn't answer. He turned in at the main gate. "The Booth grave," he said to the guards bent over a checkerboard.

"Gate closes at four," one answered.

"You coming to see Booth?" asked the other, a red-cheeked, heavyset man dressed in overalls.

"You come in now, you got to be out by four," the first repeated.

"People always coming to see Booth," said the second. "Green Mount got a lot of famous people buried here, but Booth draws the most. Still is a curiosity, I guess." The grave-keeper rose from the checkerboard. "Come on, I'll show you where he's at."

Wainwright, Shannon and the guard started up the hill through the cemetery. As they walked, the gravekeeper talked to Wainwright, telling him the lore of the graveyard while Shannon lagged behind looking at the grounds. On all sides were freshly cut flowers and grass, huge maple and oak trees and patches of clover. The grounds were lush here, a place for the living, not the dead, she thought. As she walked up the hill, she stopped to look at the tombstones. There were no skulls or crossbones on these graves, no symbols of death and retribution as there'd been in the grave-yards of New England near her college. Instead there were carved willow trees and roses cut out of stone. Death in the red earth of Maryland was marked by the gentle emblems of the old South.

As Shannon and Wainwright reached the gravesite, the gravekeeper pointed out the Booth grave on the right; then he turned and headed back down the hill. Wainwright stepped onto the grave and began pacing off the plot. It wasn't very large, about eight by eight, but according to the tombstones, there were thirteen people buried underground: the whole Booth clan gathered in last reunion. Shannon stood off under a tree and read the names on the markers. At the top of a stone obelisk, listed under "Children of" was "John Wilkes." Assassin of a President buried here simply as the son of his mother and father.

Shannon stepped carefully onto the plot. She wanted to speak to Wainwright, but as she walked towards him, she felt her feet sink into the soft earth. The ground was still wet from the morning rain, and she felt as though something were going to seep up from the graves and ooze around her. She tried to walk lightly and not stand in one spot too long. She glanced at Wainwright to see if he felt the same uneasiness, but he moved unconcerned over the graves. He was testing angles for pictures, aiming his camera first at the obelisk then at the family tombstones then at the crematorium on the crest of the hill.

Shannon backed off the plot and decided to watch from a small stone ledge while Wainwright worked. An idea seemed to be growing inside him. He knelt in front of the main grave, lining up his camera with the tombstone; he held his body and the camera perfectly still. Then without snapping a picture, he stood up and began pacing. Wainwright was not like most of the men she knew. He was intense at one moment, withdrawn the next, indifferent the next. He seemed to look on the world from a distance, to stand outside it and himself. He was certainly different from the men she'd known in Raleigh or at college or from her father, who saw everything only from where they stood.

Wainwright glanced over at her now, and for a moment he stared; then he moved to the ledge. "Come on," he said. "They'll throw us out soon. I want the late afternoon shadows."

"Where are we going?"

"There's a gardener's shack on the other side."

Shannon hopped off the wall. Wainwright started walking up the hill, and she had to double step to stay up with him. She didn't know how to know him, and she said, "You know you're not an easy person to get to know."

He glanced over at her. "I didn't know you were trying."

"We live in the same house; I've seen you twice since I moved here."

"I see you every night."

"You do?" She looked at him. He must see her from the

window, she thought. It pleased her suddenly to think of him watching her. "Emmeline says you stay in your room for months sometimes."

Wainwright frowned. "Emmeline says a lot of things."

"She also says you won't talk about yourself."

"There's nothing to talk about."

"You must come from somewhere...have a family... belong to someone."

"Do you belong to someone?"

"I have a family...a father at least and an aunt, an uncle, friends."

"Oh?"

She watched him. "What's wrong?"

He didn't answer at first, but finally he said, "People who belong don't usually come to Ruby's." Then he turned off the path and strode through the graves.

When Shannon caught up with him this time, she asked, "You don't trust me, do you?"

He answered without looking at her. "I don't trust anyone out to prove his own goodness."

"You assume that's what I'm doing?"

"Aren't you?"

She walked for a moment. When she answered, her voice was quiet. "Because you can't fit me into your imagination, don't assume I'm limited by it as well."

Wainwright turned, and he smiled. Then he pointed ahead of them. "There."

In the corner of the cemetery against the far wall was a wooden shack. Wainwright led Shannon over to it. The door was padlocked, but he took a stick from the ground the began jimmying a window open. "We'll hide here."

Shannon stared into the dank, musty space. "It's so dark in there."

"You get used to it." He raised the window. "Go on." But Shannon just stood staring inside. Finally when she didn't move, Wainwright started climbing through the window without her, and he disappeared on the other side.

"Wainwright...Wainwright?" She hoisted herself up and

saw that the ground was not so far below nor an exit too difficult and so she dropped onto the dirty wooden floor.

The room was filled with rakes and hoes and hoses, bags of fertilizer and other paraphernalia, and in the far corner was a cot with a bare mattress and a blanket wadded at the foot. Shannon stayed by the wall near the window, but Wainwright wandered about the room for a moment. Finally he turned and looked at Shannon; he didn't say anything; he just stood staring until she asked, "Have you been here before?"

"Once."

"With another girl?"

He smiled but didn't answer.

Shannon began moving along the wall. She reached out and touched the rough wooden side of the shack. Wainwright stepped over to her and put his hands on her shoulders and turned her around. "Sit down." She didn't move. He took her hand and drew her down to sit on the cot beside him. He leaned back against the wall, his legs propped up, clad in dirty jeans. He rested his arms on his knees, and he looked to her suddenly like any anonymous man on the street. She could barely see his face in the shadows, but she thought she saw him smiling, and all at once she wondered how she had let herself be brought here. "How long do we have to stay?" she asked.

"You're not afraid, are you?"

"Why did you bring me here?"

"Why did you come?"

Her dark brows moved together over her large eyes, and her expression seemed to repeat the question.

But Wainwright didn't insist on an answer. "I brought you to the cemetery because I've seen you looking inside," he said. "I wouldn't have taken you for a wanderer of graveyards."

There was something almost gentle in his tone, and for a moment she thought perhaps she hadn't been wrong to come with him, that perhaps she could trust him. "I'm not. It's just so green and quiet here. Why do you come?"

"Because it's green and quiet." He lifted his hand from the cot and placed it gently on the back of her neck and kissed her. He pressed her head against the wall, and he kissed her again. Her body was tense in his arms, but she didn't resist. She felt a quickening inside. His arms were strong and sure around her, and she felt herself drawn to this man or to her idea of this man. She let him lower her onto the narrow cot where he rested beside her on his elbow. She closed her eyes letting herself be kissed and now kissing him back. She wasn't sure where the moment was leading, but for a brief moment she suspended the question and allowed the possibility that she could exist outside time and consequence, that the moment could exist of itself. Yet stirring within her then was the suspicion that she'd begun something she wasn't prepared to finish. And stirring too was the knowledge that acts have their consequence, and no suspension of imagination can change that.

Wainwright's hand moved under her blouse and cupped at her breast. She tried to move her body from his hand, but he followed her movement, reaching for her. She pulled back. "Wainwright, please..." she whispered. But he was grasping her now. "Stop...please..."

"What's wrong?"

She breathed in deeply and opened her eyes. "I don't know you..." she said.

"Know what?" He was leaning over her, his arms holding her in a cage.

She tried to push herself up. "Anything..." She couldn't have said what she wanted to know; she only knew that she didn't know enough; she didn't know the spaces between them, and she was afraid she might lose herself inside the space. "I want you to know me too," she added quickly.

She tried again to sit up, but Wainwright wouldn't let her, and suddenly she panicked. All at once she saw herself and Wainwright from the outside, saw herself alone in a room with a man she didn't know where no one could hear her or help her. She hit at his arm to free herself. But as

57

soon as she struck him, she realized she had made a mistake. Wainwright rolled away and stood up from the cot. He began gathering his camera, and he moved over to the window now.

"I'm sorry...it's just that..." she tried.

"I'm going back," he said. "You better come too if you want to find your way out." And he climbed through the open window.

A few moments later Shannon emerged. She followed him at a distance along the back wall. She didn't know what Wainwright had expected of her; she hardly knew him, she repeated to herself. In her mind she began telling him who she was, why she was who she way, but as she neared the Booth grave and saw him, she realized he didn't care who she was. He had stopped there and was striding over the graves lining up angles for pictures as though nothing had happened. His body, lean and precise, moved with his camera as he searched for his image. Shannon stopped by the small stone ledge. She wanted to announce herself, to challenge Wainwright and show him she wasn't as naive as he thought, but she couldn't think of what to say and so she just stood watching.

Finally Wainwright called, "Come here."

"What?"

"Come here," he repeated. "I want you to lie on the grave." He pointed to the hump in the center of the plot. "I want a figure in the picture."

"On the grave?"

"Lie with your head to the stone." Shannon didn't move. "What's wrong?" he asked.

"Why do you want a picture of the grave?"

"Just lie down." But still Shannon didn't move. "The grave's historical," he said, his voice irritated now.

She eased over to the grave. Sitting on the hump, she stretched out her legs; then she leaned back and rested her head against the gravestone. But as she felt the grass and the soft earth yield to her body, she sat up. "My mother's dead, Wainwright..." she announced, beginning her explanation.

But Wainwright declared, "Christ, I don't want to know about your mother." He aimed the camera at her and began to set it into focus. "Would you take off your clothes?"

"What?"

He lowered the camera. "Would you take off your clothes please?" He adjusted the lens opening. "I want your body on the grave. Hurry before the light fades." The shadow from the hill half-covered Shannon's body, and the sun skimmed through the late afternoon haze turning the sky a soft orange.

"Can't you take me like this?" she asked now.

"I want a naked body," he said. "A virgin's naked body."

"I'm not..." Shannon started to protest, but Wainwright wasn't even looking at her. He was resetting the camera. Finally he aimed the camera at her, and he waited. Shannon glanced about the graveyard; no one was around. She wanted to prove to Wainwright that she wasn't afraid; she wanted to prove to herself that she could act beyond her own borders, and so she sat up on the edge of the grave and started pulling off her sweater. She kicked off her sneakers, took off her socks. She began to unbutton her blouse. She opened the blouse halfway, exposing the soft beginnings of her breasts. She looked up then. Wainwright was watching her now, but she stared dispassionately. He held the camera between them, and his look was so cool and detached that a shiver ran through her. She looked down at the grave then at her own naked bosom, and suddenly she grabbed her sweater and her sneakers.

"No!" she declared. "No...that's not the way it is." And she stood. She ran down the hill. She fumbled with the buttons of her blouse, and she buttoned them in the wrong holes. Wainwright threatened her; he threatened to look into her without caring who or what she was. This taking is what she feared, and this is what she thought had happened.

As she fled, Wainwright watched her, raising the camera to his eye. But he couldn't get her in focus, and he couldn't find the light he wanted in which to see her. When he climbed out over the cemetery wall that night, he still had taken no pictures.

SISSY MAMMA'S WIG

The man say, "Come here, kid." Big fat black kid what he say, but when I ask, what you say, he say, "Come here, kid."

"Whatchu want turkey?" I answer. But when he say, what you say, I say, "What you want?"

"What you doing throwing rocks at me?" he shout.

"I hit you?" I ask. "I hit you?" I want be sure I hit him before I tell him I ain't mean to hit him.

"You know you hit me," he yell. "What you throwing rocks at decent people for?"

"I'm sorry, mister," I say. "I ain't mean to hit you." Then I start to walk away. I take Sissy's arm; Sissy the little girl what always hangs around with me. She whispering, "What you doin; what you doin?"

"Sorry, mister," I say again, and I grin then pull Sissy away. She still whispering, "What you doing? Why you act so mean?" She always asking me why I act so mean. I tell her again, "Cause I hate stupid people, and nothing stupider n a white man lying in the park with his shirt off trying to get black."

Sissy don't understand though. She part white herself. Her mamma, white. Her mamma don't like me either. "Why you hang around with that fat nigger boy?" her mamma ask Sissy though her mamma hardly one to talk. Sissy don't answer her mamma. "What's the use?" she tell me. That's the way Sissy is; she don't fight back. That's why she hang around with me I guess cause I keep people from messing

61

with her, same way I keep them from messing with me. People expect me to be mean though. When you in seventh grade, weigh two hundred pounds and black, people just expect you must be mean. It easier that way really. Do what people expect, causes less aggravation. Least it keeps them from calling you, "Fat boy, tub of lard." But Sissy don't understand that either. She's still in sixth grade. Sissy don't care much about the outside of things. If people sass her—"Sissy, Sissy, what a prissy pussy,"—she just walk on by like she don't even hear them. She like her father that way. Her father, he just turn hisself off when people try to make him mad.

Sissy father nice to me. He run a garage down on Duane Street, and he let me come hang around when I want, watch him fix up cars. He never say much, and I don't say much. He just work, and I watch. Sometimes Sissy's mamma come down, and she say, "What that boy doing here?" Sissy's father say, "Leave him alone; he ain't hurting nothin." Other day Sissy's mamma come down, and she start carrying on, think I can't hear in the other room. "But he so big," she say. "He scares me. It's not natural for a child only twelve years old be that fat, ain't natural. There must be something wrong with him." She start getting after Sissy's father for letting Sissy hang around with me, and Sissy's father listen as though he thinking about what she say; then he just laugh.

"Womin, I know what wrong with you. You just scart you going get like him—fat and black. Come to think of it, you getting a mighty fat ass." And he grab her ass. She start yelling at him, but he just laugh, and she stomp away. Sissy father go back to work, pretend he working on the car, but I know he thinking about did I hear. After a while, he call me over as though he want to show me something about how to fix a radiator, but I know he just trying to make me feel good. I pretend I didn't hear, and he pretend I didn't hear, but we both know I did, and ain't nothing anyone can do to make it different.

That day when I go home from the garage, I see Sissy's

mamma sitting out on the steps. She talking to Miz Franklin, which is like talking to the whole neighborhood cause anything anyone tell Ethel Franklin going to be over the whole of North Philadelphia by suppertime. Sissy's mamma act like she don't see me coming, but when I get close, she start to whisper. I stop by the candy store, hide myself behind a tree and pretend I can't hear. Sissy mamma wait; then finally she start up again. Miz Franklin listen to her real respectful because Sissy's mamma always act like she a little better than everyone else, and people just got to believing she is. She sits there like she one of us, only she always dressed up. Her face covered with makeup that turns orange when it's hot out, and she keeps her hair all done up. She got red-blonde hair everyone say is so pretty, only I happen to know it ain't her real hair. She wear false eyelashes too and is always painting her fingernails. She worry so much about how she look, but Sissy's father right—she *is* getting fat. Actually, she a fat lady if anybody wants my opinion, only she hold on such airs, nobody say so. Now that it's hot, you can see she fat cause she starts sweating like a fat person. Her face sweats all up and turns orange, and you can just see she's having trouble breathing.

Anyway when I come down the block, I see her point to me, and I know she's telling Miz Franklin about what happen down at the garage. She quiet for a minute, but then she go on. "He always hanging around. There must be something wrong with his family," I hear her say. Her voice try to sound like she care, but I know she don't. "What do you know about his family, Ethel?" she asks Miz Franklin.

When I hear her start talk about my family, I want to tell her what my family do none of her goddamn business, but I don't say anything; I just stand there looking at the candy store window and keep listening.

"Well, Norene, I heard just the other day his mother lost her job," Miz Franklin start. Miz Franklin knitting, and she don't even look up. She talk about my mother like she talking about the weather or something. "They fired her at Elma's Beauty Salon after ten years. Put red dye instead of blonde on a customer's hair. The customer raised such hell, I hear they had to fire Cally on the spot just to get the lady quiet. Now poor Cally is out of a job though she do have a cleaning job at night so I guess she not too bad off. But she *is* hardly ever home."

"That's what I thought," Sissy's mamma say. "It's not that I want to be hard on her child, you understand; it's just that he spends so much time with my Sissy, she doesn't have a chance to make friends of her own sort, if you know what I mean."

"I do indeed," say Miz Franklin. "Sissy is a fine girl, and Roland, well, he always did cause trouble, ever since his mamma had him. I remember; I was there, you know. It was no easy time, having a baby that big. Lord, he weighed twelve pounds to begin with, and he just never stopped growing..."

Sissy's mamma go on, "Some people might say I was prejudiced against him. But I have nothing against fat people in general. It's just that Sissy is so impressionable, and his being so fat...well, it has just made that boy mean."

"Umm-umm," say Miz Franklin like she real sympathetic. "Afterall Sissy such a sweet child; she just doesn't understand the way some people are."

Sissy's mamma straightened herself on the steps now and try to look real kind. "I'm sure it's probably not Roland's fault he is the way he is," she say. "I guess it's who you're born to, and heaven knows, a child doesn't have a choice about that. And how you're raised, of course. But with Cally Jefferson never at home..."

About this time I think I'm going to slam my fist through the tree. Of course she not home, you turkey mother, I want to yell. She out cleaning houses all day and buildings at night. She do more work in one day than you ever done in your whole life. Sit around on your fat ass talking about other people...so fake...so goddamn fake like you *so* concerned when you could care less. But I don't say anything.

"Of course Cally has had her share of trouble what with Roland's daddy running off almost as soon as he see

Roland," Miz Franklin keep going on. She go on and on, and I don't know how to stop her or Sissy mamma. I think of stepping out and yelling at them, only then they just look at me all sorrow-faced and superior, like I'm only proving what they say is true. I see what I need is a plan, but I don't have one yet so I keep listening.

"I mean my heart goes out to that poor woman..." Sissy's mamma answer Miz Franklin only her voice off somewhere else, and I can tell she thinking about something else. She stop a minute; then finally she go on. "You know, Cally is quite large herself. No wonder Roland is so big. But still I guess he could lose weight if he took a mind to."

"Of course he could," Miz Franklin answer. "Anyone can do anything they want to bad enough. Why, that's what this country all about." Miz Franklin looks up from her knitting like she think she might just have said something important.

"You know..." Sissy mamma pause and consider, "I never thought of it that way, Ethel, but you're right. I mean look at my Earl. Didn't he start from nothing, and now he's got himself a garage. And some people were none too easy on him when he started if you remember, especially his marrying a white woman. Some people say I'm prejudiced, but why would I have married Earl if I were prejudiced? I'll tell you why: because Earl was a hardworking man—and I've known men to compare by—but he had a way about him, made you know he'd take care of you. His being colored was just a fact of birth."

"Never knew anyone kinder," Miz Franklin say.

"So all I'm saying about Roland is, it's certainly not on account of I'm prejudiced that I feel the way I do about him."

Miz Franklin nod her head, and Sissy's mamma sits herself back against the step now like she think the issue finally settled. She start stroking her hair. She sort of throw back her head to show herself off; then she pick up her nail polish and start at her fingernails again. She quiet for a minute; then she say, "You know I was thinking about having my hair cut again, Ethel." She tell Miz Franklin this like Miz Franklin should be so interested to know. "Earl always likes it a little shorter."

Miz Franklin all hunched up over knitting. She never got married herself, and she look more like a wore-out street horse. "Well, I don't know, Norene," she say. "You have such lovely hair; it seem a shame to cut it."

"Umm-mm," Sissy mamma sigh like this the most important decision she have to make. The truth is, her hair being a wig, it never even grow, but she always talking about getting it cut so people think it do. Sissy told me she pay $200 for that wig, say she never take it off, never let anyone see her when it not on, even Sissy's father. She even go to bed with it on. Only time she do take it off when no one else around, and then she close all the shades so no one can see in. Sissy know all this cause one day she come home from school early, walked in, and found her mamma sitting on the couch bald as a eight ball combing out her wig.

When Sissy told me her mamma bald, I nearly cracked my sides laughing, but Sissy didn't think it was so funny. She made me promise not to tell, made me swear in blood. I didn't want to give blood, but she said I had to. "Cut your-self and swear," she said. She looked so upset, I finally took a piece of glass and cut myself and swore I'd never tell. I asked Sissy what her mother look like without any hair, but Sissy got real serious then. She say her mamma just got a few strings on top, more like a baby's, but mostly she's bald. She been bald ever since she was fourteen, Sissy say, some disease or something; no one know exactly.

I asked Sissy if her father knew she bald, but when I asked that, Sissy got quiet and turned away. I told her I didn't know why she should be so upset; after all, it wasn't her hair, but I realized then maybe she was thinking she'd go bald too when she turn fourteen. It wouldn't matter to me, I said, and anyone it would matter to, not worth worrying over anyway, but that didn't seem to help. She told me she just wanted to be alone, and since I thought maybe she was going to cry, I let her.

Well, I'm standing there thinking what Sissy's mamma must look like without any hair when I hear her start up again talking about my mother. "You suppose, Ethel, Cally Jefferson has any men friends?" she asking now. "She is quite large, but you know some men like that in a woman; otherwise think how lonely she must be with only Roland for company."

When she say that, I step out from the tree. I'm about to go over and tell her what I think when all at once a plan flash into my mind. I stop a minute and think it over, and suddenly I see what I got to do. Instead of trying to stop her talking, I just walk away. I don't even bother to pass by her. In fact I go the other direction, walk all the way around the block and come back on my side. When I get back though, she already gone inside and only Miz Franklin left sitting out on the steps. Miz Franklin looking about now for someone to talk to, but I don't care anymore. I got a plan.

The next day I set my plan in motion. It take a few days, but once I make my move, it work like a charm. Sissy's mamma quit coming outside. No one notice at first, but then Miz Franklin start asking where Sissy's mamma, howcome she don't sit on the steps anymore. Miz Franklin even go knock on her door, but no one answer though Miz Franklin swear she hears someone inside sound like they crying. People say they see Sissy and her daddy come and go, but no one seen Norene Randolph since last Monday.

On Wednesday Joey Franklin—that's Miz Franklin's nephew—spot a big furry thing look sort of like a bird's nest hanging over the candy store; in fact birds flying to it and pulling out hairs. It hanging way up on a tree limb, and underneath a sign in big letters say: SISSY MAMMA'S WIG. The sight is so peculiar, a crowd start gathering to look at it, and one by one people start whispering, "That's Sissy's mamma's wig...Sissy mamma's wig." The thing is hung up out of reach of anyone, and people ask who could of put it there. The only way to get it down is to get a extra tall ladder from somewhere, and no one cares that much about it to bother finding a ladder.

Miz Franklin ask Mr. Ellison, who owns the candy store, if he isn't going to do something about it—why it's shameful to hang a woman's wig in a tree, she say; who would of done it . . . and who would have thought all this time that Norene Randolph wore a wig . . . not that there is anything wrong with wearing a wig of course, lots of women wear wigs, only Norene prided herself so much on her hair. Mr. Ellison just shrug his shoulders and say he didn't see any reason he should break his neck trying to get it down. After all, it was bringing more customers to his store than he'd had in months so he thought maybe he'd just leave it there. Nobody else thought it was any of their business so they didn't try to get it down either. The birds had sort of taken it as their own anyway. One by one they were plucking out the hairs till the wig itself was half bald. Over a dozen bird families were planning on hair-lined nests for winter thanks to Sissy's mamma.

The word spread fast about the wig. Everyone started asking who could have put it there. Some said it must have been Sissy's father punishing Sissy's mamma for something she done, but most agreed Earl Randolph wasn't that sort of man. Others said maybe it was Sissy finally got mad at her mother for carrying on so at her, but no one really believed Sissy was that mean. One person—I think it was Miz Franklin—said it must have been Norene herself done it just to get attention; she always did like attention, Miz Franklin said, but most everybody else said hanging up your own wig was a peculiar way to get attention, even for Norene Randolph. So the question was still open, who could have put it there.

The first days after the wig was hung, I stayed in the background. Everyone was talking on and on about it, and I thought it was a good joke. I stood by the candy store sucking on a Holloway bar listening to people guess at who did it. Nobody asked my opinion so I didn't tell them. Allie Jones and Joe Cranston from school came to the store three times the first day just to look at the wig and talk about how to climb the tree. Everybody knew it was a particularly hard tree to climb. I listened to them go on and on naming all the people they thought might be good enough to climb the tree when finally I said, "Ah, it don't look so hard."

They stared over at me like they were seeing me for the first time. Then Joe said, "Roland here don't think it look so hard."

"Probably not for him," Allie answered. "All he got to do is sit on a branch and the whole tree come falling down after him." They laughed then, but I didn't pay them no mind. They just ignorant, always have been. I didn't care if they called me fat—I gotten used to stupid people can't see anything but they own face—but it did get to me that they didn't think I could climb the tree. I didn't say anything though. I didn't want to give myself away.

The next day after school I went to the store again, but everybody talking so much about the wig, asking who did it, I start to get disgusted. Everyone gossip like flies around garbage here. I don't know why they think it so important. I start to get a little worried how Sissy and her father taking it. I know for a fact Sissy father been getting home late the past few nights. People not sure if he's seen the wig or not, but I figure he must know something's wrong. I mean with Sissy mamma's sitting at home bald, he must of noticed a difference. When he do come home, he always carrying a box from some beauty parlor, and in the morning when he leaves, he carry out the same box. Each night he got a different box, and each morning he carry it out again. Everyone say he probably trying to find a wig Sissy's mamma like, only natural hair wigs hard to come by these days, at least those a person can afford. That's what my mamma say.

When my mamma hear about Sissy mamma's trouble, she try to help. When I get home from the candy store Friday, I find her sitting in the chair by the telephone dialing up beauty parlors. At first I think she looking for another job so I don't pay any mind. I go over to the icebox and start making myself a sandwich; I got troubles of my own I'm trying to figure out. Allie Jones and Joe Cranston at the store when I got there today. They hanging around with they football friends, talking about the wig. When I come up, Allie stop talking, and he point to me, "Roland here think he can climb that tree," he say.

"Oh yeah?" Billy Beasley ask. "Let's see him climb the tree." I try to ignore them, but Joe Cranston start up, "Come on, Roland, climb the tree." "Yeah, Roland, climb the tree," say Allie. When I see they not going leave me alone, I turn and face them straight on.

"Your brains in your pants," I say, but Allie laughs out loud. He standing there sucking on a box of sugar daddies, and I knock the box from his hand. Sugar daddies roll all over the sidewalk, and Allie starts sputtering. He puts up his fists like he's going to fight me which is okay by me. I suck in my breath, ready to fight too, but his friends grab hold of his arms. "Aw, come on, Allie. You fight him, he might just fall on you and kill you." Allie starts laughing then, sort of nervous, and his friends start laughing; then they walk away.

I'm thinking what fools they are, and how I should of taken them all on when I hear Mamma in the living room asking about a good buy on natural hair reddish blonde. I can't figure what she doing so I listen a minute. Then I hear her say the hair not for her, and all at once I wonder if she calling up about Sissy's mamma.

When she hang up, I ask, "What you doing?"

She say she trying to help out Norene Randolph.

"Why you want to help her?" I ask. "She never helped you."

Mamma say a person has to help where he can, doesn't matter if he's helped back.

"But she don't even care about you," I tell her. "She make fun of you."

My mamma look up at me sort of sad; then she say, "Sissy, your friend, isn't she? And Earl Randolph always been nice to us. He ask me if I know of any wigs. Why shouldn't I help?"

I start pacing back and forth. I should of guessed my mamma'd do something like this. She so nice sometimes, let people walk right over her. "Cause Miz Randolph say spiteful things about you," I say.

Mamma look at me in the way she got makes me feel like I'm the one at fault. "Roland, you start acting by what other people say about you, you going be in they power your whole life."

"But, Mamma..." I argue. I don't want to tell her what Sissy's mamma say, but I see I got to stop her. I stall a minute, but then I start explaining how Miz Randolph say she don't take care of me, how she must be lonely with only me for company.

Mamma listen while I'm talking, but when I'm done, she just answer, "Sissy mamma jealous of me I guess."

"What?" I stare at her. She sitting in the chair with the slipcover tore half off, dressed in her grey cleaning uniform, and I can't think why Sissy mamma be jealous of her. But I don't say anything. I stand up and go over to the door. "I'm going outside," I say. She just nod her head. As I step into the hallway, I hear her start up again dialing the phone.

I got to get away. I hurry out towards the street, but when I get to the steps, I see Miz Franklin and some others sitting there, still talking about Sissy mamma's wig. They talking about it like they don't have anything better to occupy they time, like they don't see anything in the whole world more important. All they interested in now is what Sissy mamma's hair must really look like.

"Who cares?" I shout at them. They stop for a minute like they not sure if I'm talking to them. "Who cares?" I say again. "She bald, but who cares?" And I go down the steps without looking back. I hear them start to whisper then, and I know they wondering if it's true, and wondering if it is true, how I know. But whether it's true or not, they glad at least to have something new to chew on. As I start across the street, I hear Miz Franklin ask Miz Beasley if she think Norene Randolph really *bald*.

I go to the park. The park only place I can get away. No one bothers me there. I go over to where I like to sit, between two big rocks—my office you might say—and I try to figure why Mamma and Sissy and even Sissy father to a extent just let people go on and on about them and don't never fight back. They leave all the fighting to me, but when I do it, they look at me like I'm the one at fault.

I reach into my pocket and pull out a Almond Joy. I'm sitting there thinking when all of a sudden I hear someone coming. I look around the rock, and there Sissy herself. She surprised to see me too, but she don't say anything. She look like she been crying, and she just stands there staring at me. I offer her some candy, but she shakes her head. I think maybe she want to walk so I get up, and she follow along beside me, but still she doesn't say anything. I watch her out of the corner of my eye. She a light brown, got small brown eyes and a crooked mouth; she not very pretty, and she so shy, she doesn't have many friends. I think how nice it be if there just Sissy and me and my mamma and her daddy, and I wonder why there have to be Sissy mamma anyway.

That's when I see the man lying belly up in the park. He look more like a big piece of whale blubber than a person so I pick up a stone and throw it at him. He don't move at first so I throw another one, but then he jump up and start yelling, asking me why I'm throwing rocks at decent people. Sissy start carrying on then too, asking why I act so mean. Her face gets all screwed up like she mad.

"What's wrong?" I ask, but she doesn't answer. Her mouth is squeezed tight over her teeth, and I think maybe she's mad at me. "Well, if you don't want to tell, that's all right by me," I say. I start to walk away.

But Sissy step in front of me now, and suddenly I don't know how, she yelling at me. She never yelled at me before in her life; in fact I never heard her yell at anyone, but she yelling, "You are mean and hateful, Roland Jefferson. I didn't think you were, but people right, you spiteful and mean. You swore in blood you never tell! You swore in blood, but now everyone on the whole block talking about how my mamma bald. You was my best friend, and you told. Now I don't have *anyone* I can tell *anything* to." She gasp for breath, and I think for a minute she done, but then she start up again.

"Mamma crying all the time now saying people hate her, that's why they hung her wig in a tree. She say it's just like when she first moved here, and all these years she been trying so hard to get along. She say we got to move. Pappa say we can't move; his business here, but she say if we don't move, she going to die inside the house cause she not coming out again till the moving vans pull up to take her away. Pappa told me he'd try to work things out so we don't have to move, but now you told everyone she's bald, she'll never come out. We going to *have* to move now. How could you of done it? How could you? I hate you, Roland, I hate everyone on the whole block." And suddenly she turn and start running down the hill.

I stand there a minute like I been hit in the stomach, "Sissy..." I call finally. "Sissy, wait." But she keeps running. "Sissy...Sissy..." I start to run after her. I run all the way down the hill, but I can't catch her. I don't run too fast, and she gets further and further away. Finally I have to stop cause I can hardly breathe. "Sissy, please. I'm sorry, Sissy!" But she on the other side of the park now. I start up after her again, but I can't catch my breath, and pretty soon I don't even know where she gone.

I stand for a minute trying to figure what to do. People are staring at me like they think I must be some sort of freak flying down the hill screaming at a little girl, but I don't care. I glare back at them. I straighten myself up and stick my hands in my pockets. I start back up the hill. I go to my office where no one can see me. What Sissy say shake me up; I don't know if she mean it that she hate me and she got to move, but I know I got to do something. I sit there a long time trying to figure it out. I just sit thinking, trying to come up with a plan.

It dark by the time I get back to the block. Miz Franklin sitting on a different step now, but she still looking out over the street. There only a few other people outside. Mostly it's late, and everybody's gone home. Mr. Ellison closing up the candy store; he got one shade pulled down already, but there still some customers inside so he's selling to the last. I'm out of candy myself, but I don't go in. I stop beside the store instead. It took me a long time to figure what I got to do. At first I thought I'd find Sissy and try to tell her why I told her mamma bald, but I realize it's not something you can explain.

I wait now till all the customers go out of the store. I wait till Mr. Ellison hisself goes upstairs, till even Miz Franklin go in for the evening. Then when the street finally clear, I make my move. I set two crates from the back of the store under the tree. I take a rope from the back porch and throw it over the limb of the tree; then I climb up on the crates. I hoist myself up the rope, wiggle all around till finally I can reach the bottom limb, and I pull myself up. I lie for a minute face down on the wood. I look at the street below, but no one's there. I look up into the tree, but it's so high and dark I can't see the top. If I fall, no one even know till morning, and for a minute I wonder if my plan's the right one after all.

On Monday when I climbed the tree, I didn't think about falling, just climbed, but tonight I feel more alone, and I sit up on the limb. The branch above me at an angle, and I can't figure how I got to it the first time. I stand and hold onto the trunk the best I can; then grabbing the limb, I throw my legs around the tree and hang almost upside down. I work pulling myself around till finally I'm lying face down on the wood again, only now I'm a branch higher.

I climb the whole tree this way, belly first, and by the time I reach where I'm going, I'm sweating bad. I look up, and at the end of the branch I see what I come for. Hanging like a old used-up squirrel's nest is Sissy mamma's wig. At least what's left of it. It look more like a dead varmint to me, all fuzzy and matted down. It's so far out on the limb though, I don't know how I'm going to get it without falling out of the tree. I lie there trying to figure a way when all of a sudden I hear someone yelling up at me.

"Who's in that tree?" the person shout. I look down, try to see who it is, but the person's standing by the trunk so

I can't make him out. "Whoever you are, you come down right now or I'm calling the police," he say. I move out a little on the limb to see. "You hear me? Sarah, go call the police." When he say, 'Sarah,' I realize it's Mr. Ellison down there talking to his wife.

"It's just me, Mr. Ellison," I yell. "Roland Jefferson." But he doesn't hear me. Windows in the building next door start to open, and I see Mr. Beasley and Mr. Johnson peer out.

Mr. Ellison calls again. "All right, I've called the police," he say. "You hear me? I've got a gun down here too so you better give yourself up."

A gun! What's he doing with a gun, I want to know. I peek around the limb, and sure enough he's standing there with a shotgun aimed straight up at me. "Don't shoot, Mr. Ellison!" I yell. This is more serious than I thought. "Mr. Ellison, it's just me," I try to shout, but he doesn't hear me, and I realize I'm only whispering. I can't seem to make my voice come out any louder. "Mr. Ellison...!"

But Mr. Ellison starts counting now. I don't know what he's counting to or what will happen when he gets there, but I don't want to find out. The trouble is though I can't seem to move. I want to, but I can't make my body start down the tree. "Five...six...seven..." People begin to arrive now, and they start counting too: "Eight...nine...ten..." At first I'm afraid what's going to happen, but I realize they don't know what number they counting to either so I relax a little.

The police come next. Everyone crowds around them, and I try to hear what they saying, but I can't. Then all at once everyone looking up at me again. At least if I fall now, there be somebody there to help me. I start wondering what people'd do if they saw a two hundred-pound kid come flying through the air at them when all of a sudden two huge spotlights glare up at me.

"Hey!" I call. I try to wave them away, but they stay on, steady like a big yellow eye got me cornered. At the end of the branch I see Sissy mamma's wig also in the spotlight. It hanging there shameful and ugly, and I remember why I climbed the tree in the first place, and I start trying to figure a way to get it down.

From below someone shout, "Why, it's Roland Jefferson in that tree. What you doing up there, Roland?" I recognize the voice as Miz Franklin's. "You come down here this instant," she say like climbing down a tree is the easiest thing in the world. I don't listen to her now though. I got to get the wig. I look about for a stick; then I start poking at the wig. I hear people whispering: "What's he doing? What's he doing?" Then Miz Franklin shout, "Roland, think of your mamma!"

Why should I think of my mamma, I wonder, but then I realize Miz Franklin probably think I'm going to fall and kill myself. The thing is though, I don't feel so scared anymore. I start inching out on the branch. I know I must look like some kind of sideshow hanging upside down, but I don't care. I reach out, and with one swipe, I hook the wig off the tree. When people see what I got, they go, "Oooo!" and all of a sudden someone start clapping. Then more and more people begin clapping.

I start down the tree real easy, holding the wig in my teeth. When I get to the bottom limb, Mr. Beasley and Mr. Johnson help me out. Everybody comes up, starts congratulating me, patting me on the back, saying how brave I am. I can't figure it out, but I don't say anything. I stand there holding the wig behind my back, trying to hide it. I don't know why everybody think saving a wig such an important event.

The police come up, start asking me all sorts of questions, and I try to answer the best I can. Next Joe Cranston and Bill Beasley step over talking about what kind of knot I must have used to climb a tree with a rope; they talk as though they knew how to climb the tree all along, but I don't say anything. Then off to the back of everyone I see Sissy. At first I expect her to step up, congratulate me too, but she doesn't. I keep my eyes on her while Joe and Bill going on and on.

Finally she walks over to me, but instead of saying anything, she just takes the wig out of my hand. I start to say something myself, but she turns and without a thank you or nothing, she starts off towards her house. Suddenly I feel empty inside, in spite of everyone saying what a hero I am, and I wonder why I climbed the tree in the first place and what was the use.

Early the next morning, Saturday morning, a van pull up at Sissy's house. I happen to be up cause I can't sleep. I'm sitting by the window eating pancakes when I see two men go into Sissy's building. The next thing I see is Sissy's father coming out. He's talking with the man, and they all shaking their heads together. At first it doesn't sink into me what's happening. I just watch them, curious to see what comes next. But then I see one of the men carry a chair out of the building and start setting it in the truck. All at once it dawn on me Sissy moving. I push up from the table and go over to the window. I start walking back and forth.

From the doorway my mamma steps into the room. At first I don't see her, but then she say, "Roland, what *is* the matter?" She standing there in her bathrobe, barefoot. I glance over at her then look back out the window. She follow my eyes. "Why, who's moving?" she ask.

"Sissy," I say. I keep walking. My mamma can see I'm upset, but she doesn't make notice.

"I wonder where they moving," she say.

I don't answer. I try to figure if it's too late to stop them. I never meant for things to go this far, and I can't figure how they did. I see another man come out carrying another chair, and all at once I feel panic inside. "I didn't mean to do it," I say. I look over at Mamma. "I didn't mean to." She stare at me like she can't figure what I'm talking about. "I didn't know everyone take a wig so serious."

Mamma get quiet for a minute; then she ask, "Roland, you the one hung that wig in that tree?"

I nod my head. I expect her to get mad at me, start lecturing me on Christian kindness, but all of a sudden she burst out laughing. I'm so surprised, I almost forget what's happening outside. She try to get serious, but she keep laughing. "Lord, Roland, what a thing to do," she say. "How'd you get that wig in the first place?"

Seeing Mamma laugh like that make me relax a little. I start thinking maybe everything's not so bad after all, and I start telling her how I sneaked into Sissy's house one morning, and when Sissy mamma take her wig off and go to the bathroom, I grab it and run out. Mamma's face get more serious then.

"Roland, I'm ashamed of you breaking into other people's houses," she say. "But I'm glad you told me. Why, Earl Randolph been worried sick the last few days. He think the neighbors done it who used to try to worry Norene out of the neighborhood. That's why everybody been carrying on so. They wondering if it one of them did it bringing back the old days. That wig hanging in the tree...well, it was just a bad sign nobody knew how to read."

I stare at my mamma; she looking out the window now. I had no idea so much behind what I did. Across the street Sissy father's still talking to the moving men and Sissy's mamma out now too. She all dressed up in a fancy purple dress with ruffles around the collar. She have a purple turban round her head. She holding Sissy by one hand and holding a hat box in the other. Sissy wearing a blue and white dress with white Sunday shoes. Only one not dressed up is Sissy's father; he standing there in old slacks and a undershirt.

My mamma go into the bedroom. I hear her in the closet; then almost as soon as she's gone in, she out again wearing her print housecoat. She tells me to dress and meet her across the street. She doesn't say why, but I see by the way her face is set, she got a direction in her I better not try to argue.

Outside I wander up and sort of stand behind my mother. I can't tell if she's told yet or not what I did, but nobody's looking at me so I guess she hasn't. I glance at Sissy who still being held onto by her mother, and I can see she been crying. Her father doing most of the talking now. As I start to listen, I realize he telling mamma how I climbed the tree last night and saved Miz Randolph's wig. I forgot to tell my mother that, and by the way she nodding her head, I can see she impressed. Sissy mamma doesn't say anything. She just stand stiff as a statue, holding her head so high I think she must be cramping her neck. I glance again at Sissy out of the corner of my eye; she looking at me too, and for the first time since yesterday, I think maybe we be friends again if only my mamma won't tell.

Mr. Randolph start explaining next how Sissy mamma ordered the van today without telling him, but when he say that, Sissy mamma speak up for the first time. "Well, I won't stay in a place where people act so mean," she say. She address herself to my mamma, only she doesn't look at her. This the first time she ever talked to Mamma directly I can remember, and she look uncomfortable like she not real sure of herself after all. Seeing her this way with a scarf tied up over her bald head and neighbors watching from the street, I view her a little different than I did. She don't seem so high flown but more like she's scared people won't like her. "Any neighborhood allow people to do what they done to me...well, I don't want my child growing up there."

My mamma reach out and touch Sissy mamma's arm like it the most natural thing to do, and she say, "You know, Norene, I heard it was some kids from the other block did that. Everybody's been feeling so terrible about what happened; we do wish you'd think again and stay."

Sissy mamma look at my mamma. "It was a spiteful thing to do," she say.

My mamma nod her head. "It was."

"No reason a person has to put up with such treatment."

"No, there not. But we wish you'd stay."

Sissy mamma smooth down the ruffles around her collar. "Well, I don't know..." she say. "You think it was the kids?" When she ask that, I know she going to stay, and my mamma know too.

"I'm sure of it," Mamma answer. "You know how kids are getting these days."

"I do indeed," Sissy mamma say like Mamma opened

a subject she been giving a lot of consideration to. "It's hard for Sissy to make decent friends."

Mamma nod. "Now that's the truth, isn't it? That's why I'm grateful everyday Sissy and Roland such good friends."

Sissy mamma pause a minute and stare over at me. I can tell by the way she raise her chin and lower her eyes, she trying to decide on me right there. I stand up straight and try to look like what a good friend supposed to look like. "Well...I guess Roland is a good boy," she say, "I mean he did climb that tree." I don't say anything, just nod my head and keep looking like a good friend. "Yes, Sissy lucky too, I guess."

Sissy father impatient by now cause he know every minute they out there talking, the men with the van making more money. He ask if that mean he can tell the men to go.

"Well, maybe we should stay on..." Sissy mamma say like she still thinking about it. "I mean if all the good folks move out, who's left?"

My mamma nod in agreement. Sissy mamma turn to the men and say she guess they not moving today after all. I glance at Sissy. She still not smiling, but the way she look at me out the corner of her eye, I can tell everything going to be all right between us. As Sissy father start to pay the men, my mamma motion to me it's time to go, and we head back across the street.

When we get to the apartment, I set about cleaning up the breakfast things right away so Mamma don't have to tell me. She go into the other room and start dressing for work. I'm at the sink thinking I'm glad Sissy going to stay but worrying now if Bill Beasley really mean what he said about tree climbing Sunday when suddenly Mamma laugh out loud.

From the other room she call to me. "You know, Roland," she say, "you some good company." Then she laugh again. "Yes, you and me are some good company."

EURLANDA'S BOX

"I built the box, Mamma, and there no way you going make me come out. Hear that! I have got to have some privacy. Only this four by four box. It don't take up much room, but it's mine, you hear. I'm staying in here just as long as I please, and I'll come out when I please and talk to who I please. About time you see I'm a lady almost, and ladies have got to have privacy."

The box fell silent. Eurlanda sat inside in the middle of the bedroom floor. "So you leave me alone. All you leave me alone, and don't no one dare knock over my box again."

Again the box was silent. Eurlanda heard her mother's heavy oxfords in the doorway and the bare feet of her younger brothers and sisters hurrying past. She curled up in the corner of the box and began looking at herself in the double-sided red plastic mirror she'd bought at the drugstore in town. Her dark eyes peered out above broad cheekbones. She licked her finger and squeezed her eyelashes curled.

"You pretty, you know that, only you got to start acting like you look." That's what he'd said to her. First man ever said anything to her outside B.J. and Chick and they weren't even men hardly. She was pretty. She could see that now. She intended to be prettier too so that he'd take her out, only he was leaving soon. Charlie'd told her that. Pinter, he don't stay long in no place. Just drifting north he reckoned like anyone else with any sense these days. No one but a ground chewing worm live off this land any more. Even then he get indigestion, Charlie said, even the worm get in-di-

ges-tion. But she'd keep Pinter here; she would if she could
or she'd go with him because she was going to die herself
if something didn't happen and happen fast. She was fourteen, and she was living the same way she'd lived all her
life and nothing, nothing ever changed. Things only got
older.

Pa was getting older, old early in his life, ever since Lisa
Ann had run away. Then Jacob Junior had left, and now she
was about to leave though she didn't know how. She didn't
want to leave Pa, but she couldn't wait around for him to
die; she'd die first. Mamma said she was his favorite next
to Lisa Ann. Lisa Ann was his first. But then one day, August
17, 1954, Lisa Ann and the store manager at Woolworth's
where Lisa Ann worked at the luncheonette, got into his
red Chevrolet and drove off leaving everyone else behind,
leaving three old ladies waiting at the counter for tuna fish
sandwiches and leaving the manager's wife and two kids
in the apartment upstairs. First few months she was away,
Lisa Ann sent Eurlanda postcards from Houston and from
Dallas. She wrote Mamma a letter that had made her cry.
But then she quit writing. It'd been over a year now since
anyone'd heard from Lisa Ann. No one talked about her any
more. No one knew where she was.

After she left, Pa drank himself sick. Then one afternoon
he called the children one by one into the shed at the edge
of the field, and he beat them with his belt. He told them
if they ever ran off like Lisa Ann, he'd come after them. He
was mean drunk that day, and his face was red and twisted.
Eurlanda had been afraid of him, but she'd also seen in his
face something that had made her want to cry for him.

When Mamma came home and found the children all
huddled in the kitchen, when she saw the welts on Martha's
back, she'd nearly gone crazy herself. She went for the gun.
She threw Pa out of the house. He stayed away more than
a month before she let him back in. She made him swear
on God's Bible in front of all the children that he'd never
drink again. He took the oath, but he still drank though
Eurlanda never again saw him drunk. That was two years

ago. Now instead he was real quiet. The only time he perked up these days was when Eurlanda was around, when they'd play dominos after dinner or talk on the back steps.

But Pa was sick now. Eurlanda didn't know what was wrong with him. She'd seen the doctor come almost every day this week. She didn't want to leave, but she had to get on with her own life, didn't she?

Eurlanda smoothed her dust brown hair around her face and pulled the front piece over one eye. The day her mother saw her wearing her hair like that and saw her lips red with Lisa Ann's old lipstick and her eyes made up, she'd almost hit her.

"I got one daughter a tramp; I ain't having two. You been raised in a Christian home, and you getting your hair shaved off before I see you prancing around like that again. You going straight to the devil if you don't watch out." Her mother had rubbed her eyes and mouth so hard that she nearly pushed them clean through the other side of her head. But Eurlanda reckoned she wouldn't go to the devil, leastwise not any time soon because she had a lot she meant to do first.

She curled her hair around her finger and practiced winking in the mirror, winked straight through the mirror past the box at Pinter, and he winked back, and she was kissing him, all the time kissing him hard, and he was saying more, baby, now kiss me back, and she knew how without ever doing it before, and she kissed him back so deep that he hugged her to him and wouldn't let go until she promised to go away with him. Why, Mr. Pinter, I hardly know you, she'd say, only then he'd ask why she'd kissed him like that and she'd laugh, did you think I kiss good? Oh, baby, you kiss like no one ever kissed before. You don't go with me, I'll die for wanting you. Then I'll have to go with you, won't I, and she would too, just like that, not even tell her mother where she was going but shoot out into life and find what it was all about.

It was about more than farming dust. She knew that. It was about more than working in the fields or sitting in school with a bunch of dumb kids didn't know half what she did. She aimed to know even more too. She aimed to get smart, but not from any sixty-year-old teacher talking about how radios changed the course of civilization. She was getting smart from herself. When she left, she'd send Pa postcards from all the places she and Pinter went. Houston. Dallas. Chicago. New York. Big color postcards, the kind he kept in his cigar box at the top of the closet. She'd send him a dozen cards, and he'd be glad she was going out into life. She'd tell him she wasn't running away from him; she was just running towards life. He'd understand; she knew he'd understand. After all, hadn't he told her he'd done the very same thing when she was only a baby? He'd run away too and tried to catch life. Only finally he'd come home because he had to take care of her and Mamma. Well, she was feeling that same kind of flood inside right now. It was churning and splashing and lapping, and if she didn't do something quick, it would bust her wide open. She was going to do something with her life; she knew that, and she knew it was going to be good and better than anything Lisa Ann or her mother or father or anyone before her had done, but she didn't know what it was, and inside it hurt and tingled all at the same time. She thought maybe it would have something to do with Pinter, but then if he was only going to be a drifter, maybe it wouldn't be with Pinter.

So here she sat with two books, magazines, a mirror, tweezers, a half-used tube of lipstick. And here she would stay until she'd decided what to do with her life.

Eurlanda read most of the morning. That is she read and plucked her eyebrows, plucked her eyebrows and then read, then thought about Pinter then plucked her eyebrows. She used Tricia's tweezers for Tricia had told her she had to work on herself if she wanted to get a man like Pinter. "You got soulful eyes, Lani," Tricia said, "but nobody can see 'em with those two catipillars meeting across them." Tricia had been Lisa Ann's best friend, and she'd taken it on herself to school Eurlanda now that her sister had run away. Tricia gave her copies of *Glamour* and *Modern Screen*, and Eurlanda studied the pictures inside to see how she was supposed to look and be though it was clear to her, people in those magazines had never even been on a farm and probably didn't know a place like Redcreek, Texas existed.

She closed the magazines and picked up one of the books instead. She imagined herself as the lady on its cover holding a fan with two men leaning over each shoulder. She was sitting there as if she always had men leaning over her shoulder. A small heart hung around her neck for all the hearts she'd taken because she had soulful eyes. She had decided she'd read this book *Portrait of a Lady* she'd gotten at Mabel Whatley's garage sale. Mabel Whatley had been an English teacher in Corpus Christi. Eurlanda helped her starch clothes Saturdays so Miss Whatley had let her choose free from the odds 'n ends table at the sale. She was counting on this book to tell her how to be a lady so by the time she was fifteen in two months, she would be ready.

She'd leave then, when she was fifteen and smart and a lady. She couldn't tell anyone what she was planning though because everyone still thought she was just a kid in blue jeans working in the fields. But she had to work in the fields. Who else was there? Ever since Lisa Ann had run away and Jacob gone and Papa sick. There was only Roper and herself and Munroe. John Jack came out some, but he was just a kid, and Martha when she came out was more trouble than help. Pa tried to help, but lately she and Roper ended up doing his work so most of the time he stayed in the house figuring. Bookkeeping, he said, going over figures all day long, the same figures over and over as if by looking at them he was going to make them come out different.

It was hard times, Mamma'd told her. And in hard times you just had to hold on. Well, it was always hard times, Eurlanda said. All she remembered was hard times, and she couldn't wait her life for times to change. Papa and Mamma were going to have to find someone else to do her work because she wasn't coming out of her box till the lady in her learned to come out first. She plain couldn't ask Mamma any of the things she wanted to know. Mamma'd been so high-strung lately, she couldn't ask her anything. This

morning Mamma'd slapped her for no reason at all. Ever
since Pa'd gotten sick, Mamma'd been meaner than a cat.
Besides Mamma just plain never was a lady. She thought
being a fine lady had something to do with the devil, and
Eurlanda wanted no more Sunday preaching. She was
giving up that too. Giving up Sunday and school and picking and just about everything had anything to do with Redcreek. She was going North, but she had to learn what she
needed to know quick before Pinter left.

Pinter had come into town two months ago. Nobody
knew where he came from or who he was or why in the
world he would come to Redcreek, but he came just the
same. There was something about Pinter Eurlanda liked,
something that made her feel good inside: the way he talked
to her and made her feel easy about talking back when before
she could hardly talk to men. He just walked up and sat
down beside her when she was on the steps of the hard-
ware store and asked her name and how long she lived in
Redcreek. Then he asked if she ever thought of leaving. She
was pretty, wasn't she, and wasn't there a lot outside of Redcreek she'd never seen. She'd been to Dallas once she told
him and to Corpus. He laughed when she said that, and
then he told her about New York and Chicago and San
Francisco.

Why'd you come here, she'd asked, and he said he was
chasing a dream. Ain't no dreams here, she answered, and
he'd laughed again. That was when he told her how pretty
she was and if she'd act like she looked, she would win all
the boys around. She'd dropped her eyes. "Serious, yours
is just about the prettiest face I've seen in all the places I've
been." He wiped dirt off her cheek with his hand, and the
way he looked at her and let his other hand fall between
her legs, she knew he wanted to touch more than her cheek.
But Mr. Lucas came out of the store then, and Pinter'd moved
away. She'd smiled at him, and he'd winked back, and they
didn't say any more that day.

The next day that was when she'd combed her hair down

over her eye and used Lisa Ann's lipstick, only when she went to town that day, Pinter wasn't there. She walked all over and even asked Charlie at the drugstore had he seen Pinter.

"Drifter like that...he'll be leaving soon. Why you want to know anyway?" Charlie'd stared hard at her as if he suspected something. "What you know about Pinter?"

"Nothing, nothing," she said quickly. "I just seen him; that's all." Charlie watched her, and she flushed. She pretended to be looking for a magazine; then she hurried out of the store.

What if Pinter had left already? She thought of that now. She closed her book and began pulling her eyebrows harder and faster; then she opened the book and read as quickly as she could, pushing the words into her head, squinting at the effort.

She'd been reading all day it seemed, at least as long as she'd ever read in one place before. She'd hid in the box this morning after her mother had slapped her. All she'd done was sneak into her father's room to peek at him. He'd been in bed with the shades drawn all week, and no one but her mother was allowed in. She and Roper had tried to peer through the windows outside, but they couldn't see anything.

"Pa's dying," Roper had told her.

"He is not," she'd declared.

"Is too," Roper said like he knew.

"Is not! Don't you ever say that again!" And she'd threatened Roper. Roper'd hushed up then, but after that she had to see for herself. She had crept into her father's room that morning. The shades were drawn, and the room was dark in spite of the bright sun outside. The room stank. As she moved towards the bed to see her father, she realized the smell was coming from him. She stopped. From the foot of the bed she whispered, "Papa...I'm here...Papa?"

But her mother had come in then. She'd marched over to Eurlanda, and without saying a word, she grabbed her arm and ushered her into the yard where she shook her till

Eurlanda's face turned red. "Don't you go into that room again!" she yelled.

"Why not?" Eurlanda had asked.

"Don't sass me, girl!" And she'd slapped her right across the face. She'd never done that before. Well, Eurlanda would show her. She'd go into town tonight, and she'd find Pinter and make sure he didn't leave without her.

It was dark as Eurlanda crept along the back fence holding her dress in her fist so she wouldn't snag the hem. She crept past the barn into the empty fields; then she hurried towards the road. The town's lights spilled bits of words into the night: Coca Cola red and yellow flashed beside Charlie's Drug. Eurlanda rushed towards the lights. She would see Pinter at Charlie's; she could see him already as he first noticed her, could see them running off together behind Mr. Lucas' garage and talking and then kissing. She'd sit on the grass with him, her head resting against his shoulder, and they'd count the stars till he'd stop counting and look at her. He'd stroke her hair and tell her how pretty she was and how very different she was from the girls in New York and Chicago. That'd be when he'd try to kiss her, and she would let him. Slowly they'd lie back together and look at the stars and kiss and kiss and kiss until he'd say she had to come away with him that very night or he'd go crazy without her. She didn't know what she'd say then when he asked her to run away, but she supposed she would go.

When Eurlanda got into town, she went to Charlie's and slipped unnoticed into the store behind the newspaper racks. Unnoticed, that is, until Mr. Gregory exclaimed, "Why look at Lani Crammer!" And all the men at Charlie's Saturday night poker game turned to stare as if they'd never seen a girl before. What in the world was she doing in town all dressed up, Mr. Gregory wanted to know between chomps on his tobacco.

"Don't she look like a lady? Think she come to see

Pinter," Charlie betrayed.

"Pinter? Why Pinter left town just this morning, heading north like we figured." Mr. Lucas winked.

"He sure did," Mr. Gregory smiled. "Seem to me he was running fast, wearing some tar and feathers too."

"She gone on Pinter?" Mr. McAndless asked.

No, she was not gone on Pinter. What do you mean tar and feathers?

"Don't blame a pretty girl like you falling for Pinter," Mr. McAndless consoled. "But he too old, and he ain't the right sort for you."

What you mean tar and feathers?

"Pinter been taking advantage our young girls round here," Mr. Lucas said.

What girls?

"Tricia Bell for one," Charlie answered. "Her pa caught Pinter out on Buella Road with Tricia last night. Pinter lucky he didn't get buckshot from what I hear he caught them at. Gertrude hadn't called the Committee to take charge, Chilton would of shot him sure."

Why didn't Eurlanda go after Billy Bob, Mr. Lucas wanted to know. "Good boy, Billy Bob. Strong too."

She wasn't after no boy. She didn't have time for boys. What had Mr. Bell caught them at, and had Pinter really gone? Only she quit asking out loud.

"Well, you should start looking at boys," Mr. McAndless said. "You ain't getting none too young. Problem is boys round here never seen you all dressed up. Tell you what I'll do. I'll get my Willie to come by and see you; I'll tell him how pretty you look tonight."

She didn't want no boys coming by bothering her; she had things to do, important things. "Don't you dare say nothing to Willie!" she declared.

"Now don't you go getting all huffed up; no sense ruining that made-up face, pouting and all..."

They laughed then. They all laughed, slapped their knees and wheezed like horses. Tar and feather a man then wheeze like horses.

"Just give me Pa's medicine," Eurlanda ordered. "I come for the medicine."

"I don't recollect your ma asking for no new medicine," Charlie said. "Maybe I just give her a call, see what she want. How your Pa anyway? Doc say he pretty sick."

"He awright. No, don't call. Never mind. I got to go; I'm going." And she left. She didn't say anything as she ran out of the store, but she heard Mr. Gregory laugh out loud again, and she knew they were all laughing at her and would always laugh at her and would never let her go.

Whop! Bang! Bang whop! "Damn you, Roper. Stop that!" Eurlanda shouted from her box. Whop! Bang! Whop! "Roper Crammer, you hear me! You quit throwing them cherry bombs. You think you can make me come out of my box. Well, you cain't, but when I do, you going wist you never seen me. You..." Bangwhopbang! "What's wrong with you, boy, can't you hear me? Ain't you got no feelings? MA-A-A! You tell Roper to leave me alone or I'm going to beat his ass off..." Bang bang and whop bang! "All right, you asked for it!"

Eurlanda struggled inside her crate of rough boards and nails. She pushed at the side to lift the box off her, but it slipped from her hands and crashed to the floor, breaking her mirror. Roper laughed. "You shut up!" she shouted. And then she stood, forcing the box up with her broad shoulders and casting it off. She lunged at Roper, who shot out from under her arm. She lunged again, but again he darted away, laughing in a high shriek. He was only twelve, lanky and more nimble than she.

"Think you so smart making me come out. Think you so smart! Well, you ain't cause I'm still going to be a lady; I'm going be a lady spite what you do, spite what anyone in the whole world do, I'm going to make me a lady."

She sat in the middle of the floor then, and she started to cry. She sobbed so hard that even Roper stood still and stared at her. Slowly he began to pick up the remnants of the cherry bombs, and her turned the box rightside up. "I'm sorry, Lani," he said. "Lani, I'm sorry..." He backed slowly out of the room.

Eurlanda just sat there. "Ah go to the devil!" she said. She sat on the hardwood floor and stared into the cracks between the wood. There were bobby pins and a chewing gum wrapper and a penny wedged into the crevices. She looked across the room. It was a mess. Martha's clothes were heaped on her orange crate and Junior's and Roper's dirty socks and comic books were lying all over their corners. Mamma was going to yell at her for the mess. Why couldn't she keep this room clean, she'd ask. She had to learn to take care of the place; otherwise no man ever going want to marry her. Do this, do that. Mamma made her do everything just because she was the oldest.

But yesterday Mamma'd slapped her. Eurlanda had been so startled, she didn't even cry. She and Mamma both just stood there staring at each other; then Eurlanda had pulled her arm free and run off behind the house. That was where she'd found the box. She'd hammered it together in the room, and Mamma didn't dare stop her. Even today Mamma hadn't tried to make her get out.

Eurlanda stared into the fields through the broken screen. The dust was blowing up again. The fields were dry and the crop brown and baked out. In the doorway flies hissed in circles as if they couldn't decide to come in or go out. At the far end of the field the old shed rattled in the wind. Only two sides of it still stood, two weather-beaten boards held together by rusted nails. Eurlanda remembered the year her father'd built that shed. They had picked so much cotton that year, they needed extra space to store it. Eurlanda'd been nine then. She was the only one her father let help him the day he built it. She knew how to stay out of his way, how to give him the nails when he needed them then step back. He'd taken special pride at having to build extra space for his crops. We're going to make it now, he'd told her; just you wait and see. We're going to make it.

But that year had been the only year they'd used the shed. The next year the drought began; Mamma had the twins the next year too, and then two years later Lisa Ann had run away. Eurlanda had forgotten all about the shed. She looked at it every day when she went into the fields—they didn't even plant that far out anymore—but she'd quit seeing it a long time ago.

She picked up Tricia's tweezers now and dug into the crack in the floor and fished out the dull copper penny. Stuffing the penny in her pocket, she took the tweezers and her book, and she ran towards the shed.

It was past suppertime when Eurlanda came home. Her mother was waiting for her in the kitchen doorway. Her mother's heavy, dimpled arms hung limp at her sides, and her eyes were fixed on some point out in the fields.

"I been at the shed, Ma." Eurlanda started defending herself right away. "Don't get mad cause I've been thinking. If I'm going to stay around here, and I'll stay for Pa, then I got to have a place..."

But before Eurlanda could explain how she was going to rebuild the shed for herself and put a window in it and put cotton sacking on the floor, her mother drew her into her apron, and she pushed Eurlanda's head onto her shoulder. All the anger and frenzy seemed drained out of her body.

"Your pa's dead," she said. "We looked everywheres for you..." Her fingers curled tightly into Eurlanda's hair. "He passed a hour ago."

HISTORY
LESSON

Little Rock, 1956

Joe Ward was sitting at the dining room table transferring students' names from roll cards into his gradebook. Elise, a junior in high school where her father taught history, was folding new book covers over her books. "I didn't say you don't develop a perspective, a thesis of cause and effect, but not judgment," Mr. Ward declared. "Most people judge the past by standards which don't apply." Mr. Ward was in the middle of a master's thesis at the university and often discussed his ideas with his daughter.

"But if no one judges, then history's only meaningless facts," Elise argued.

Joe Ward smiled; he took pleasure in his daughter's developing ability to reason. "But there's a difference between judgment and perspective..." He was about to tell her the latest distinction he'd come to see when Tommy Ward strode through the doorway. He was a large, well-built boy, half a head taller than his father and at least a foot taller than his sister. He had alert blue eyes, a slightly crooked nose, and a smile which prompted others to smile back at him.

Mr. Ward continued without glancing up. "One is a sword which dismembers; the other, a sheath." He had come to this metaphor in his writing and now tested it out loud for the first time.

Tommy leaned over the table and poured a glass of lemonade. "What do you think, Tommy?" Elise asked.

Tommy smiled as though his smile were answer enough.

93

"You and Dad never change," he said.

"What *do* you think, Tommy?" Mr. Ward persisted.

Tommy continued smiling, but his body stiffened as he sipped his lemonade. "I think I don't know what the hell you're talking about." He cut himself a piece of the cake Mrs. Ward had set out on the table.

Elise's blue eyes narrowed. "Well, it's only a theory," she dismissed.

"A rather important theory," her father noted, "for anyone interested in history and ideas."

Tommy didn't answer. He stared at the platter rather than his father; he stuffed the wedge of cake into his mouth. Elise moved over to make room for him, but Tommy remained standing. "Did Tommy tell you he was named captain of the defensive squad yesterday?" Elise asked.

"No, he didn't tell me." Mr. Ward peered over the top of his wire glasses. He was a small man with dark brown hair and sharp features. He didn't look like his son except that he too was handsome, but his own looks were more deliberate. He was clean-shaven and groomed down to his fingernails. The smell of soap and cologne and starched shirts hovered about him and was almost strong enough to overwhelm the ever-present smell of tobacco. Mr. Ward was a chain smoker. He tried to hide this fact from his students for he disapproved of his own habit, and he took his duty to his students as seriously as he took himself.

"Didn't you think I'd be interested?" he asked. Tommy didn't answer. "I only object when football interferes with your studies."

"Are we going to go through that again, Dad, because I heard it already."

"I'm not going *through* anything. But nobody ever got into college winning football games."

"Oh yeah?" Tommy answered.

Mr. Ward ignored the comment. He turned the page in his grade book and resumed writing. Elise looked away. Her eyes, rimmed with dark lashes, peered down at the paper in front of her.

"Don't take it so seriously, Lise," Tommy said. "I don't."

Mr. Ward frowned. "Maybe that's the problem."

"I didn't come in here to fight, okay? In fact I came to tell you about a great opportunity I've been given." He glanced sideways at his father, who looked up now. "You know Buck Davis?" Tommy asked.

"The Negro man down at the garage."

"Yeah. Well, Buck has an old Harley Davidson he needs to sell. His family's got some sort of trouble, and he needs to raise cash quick; he said if I can give him fifty dollars by Saturday, he'll let me have it, and I can pay him the rest out of my salary each month. I was wondering if I could borrow the fifty just till I get paid."

"What sort of trouble?"

"I don't know. I get paid next Thursday."

Mr. Ward took off his glasses and set them on the table. "If you owe me fifty dollars, how are you going to pay Mr. Davis his first payment?"

Tommy thought for a moment. "I'll get a second job."

"Plus the job you already have?"

"I'm not afraid of hard work." Tommy smiled; his face was expectant.

"Plus football?"

"It'll be tough."

"And school? Does school fit into this scheme?"

His smile began to fade as he saw the outlines of his father's logic. "It's a real opportunity, Dad."

"No, Tommy," Mr. Ward said, "a motorcycle is not an opportunity. A job may be an opportunity; a college education is an opportunity, but a motorcycle is a means of transportation." Mr. Ward looked pained to have to explain again these values he insisted upon, values which he even sensed denied his son and their possibilities of closeness, but which he was unable to yield. In a nervous tic of his eye and a slackening line of his jaw he seemed almost to acknowledge his own limitation.

"So you won't give me the money?"

"If Mr. Davis needs a loan..."

"I'm not talking about charity for Buck; I'm talking about buying a motorcycle...I'll pay you interest."

"I don't want interest. You're missing the point."

"The point? What point?" Tommy's face flushed as he strained to control the anger suddenly upon him. "The point, Dad, is that you wouldn't give me an extra lousy dime if I were starving on your doorstep. You've never given me anything that didn't fit into *your* policies and points. There is always a point, some point I'm just too stupid to see." Tommy shoved away from the table. "Well, don't worry. I won't ask for your help again."

Elise rose towards her brother, not directly so that Tommy or her father noticed, but her body lifted and part of her followed Tommy out the front door onto the porch where he stood for a moment before he plunged into the bright afternoon sun like a swimmer into a pool.

The dining room was suddenly quiet. For the first time Elise heard pans rattling out in the kitchen; she heard the droning of a radio talk show, and she realized her mother was out there. She couldn't help but have heard the argument, yet she remained on her side of the door. Elise wished her mother would have come in and tried to make peace, but she never did. She always let Tommy and her father have their way; then she made up to each of them separately, secretly.

Elise began stacking her books on the end of the table, which served as a desk as well as an eating space for her family. She opened her math book and began copying out her homework problems. She avoided her father's eyes. She never knew what to say after the battles between her father and her brother. She understood why her mother stayed in the kitchen for she and her mother were bonded to these two men who fought each other constantly. Yet, for a long time she had considered her mother a coward.

Mr. Ward reached over and touched Elise's hand. "I don't like to say no," she said; his voice was soothing. "Tommy doesn't understand that. He takes it personally." Mr. Ward gathered up his registration cards. "Tommy's always equated being given things with being loved. Even when he was a little boy, the first thing he'd do when I got back from a trip was go into my suitcase to see what I'd brought him. If I didn't have a present, he'd pout all day. You were never that way. You were always just happy to see me."

"Maybe Tommy needs things more than I do."

"No..." Her father put back on his glasses and put out his cigarette. "No...it's not a question of need; it's a question of values. Tommy wants for himself first; that's what I object to."

Elise stared out the screen and tried to see where her brother had run, across the street, into the sun. "I don't think you're being fair," she said. "You'd have given me the money if I asked."

"But you don't ask; that's the point," Mr. Ward said. "You never ask so I don't mind giving you things. But a motorcycle would be another distraction, another reason not to study. Even if he had the money, Tommy hasn't earned a motorcycle."

Elise squinted at her father. She rubbed her head for it suddenly ached. A crescent of dark hair fell around her face. Her features were sharp; she had a roman nose, pointed chin and small, intense eyes. "I don't know," she answered.

Her father began stacking his cards and books. He set his pen and pack of cigarettes on top of his grade book. "If you don't have values, you'll be taken along with the worst of what's in the world," he said. "You, Elise, have values. And you have transcendence. You don't get fooled by the things of the world. Tommy doesn't have transcendence. Perhaps I shouldn't say that of my own son, but that's what it comes down to: transcendence. You remember that."

Her father stood then with his books under his arm. He went into a small alcove off the living room where he shut the louvered doors he'd installed himself. He set his books on the floor and pulled his four years' old master's thesis onto the desk. He would sit there with the thesis in front of him as he did every evening until dinner and try to refine his perspective on the history before him.

Elise had worked only a third of her math problems when she heard voices in the kitchen. According to the maple leaf clock on the wall, an hour had passed, but she hadn't been able to concentrate. She looked up now to listen. She recognized the voices as those of Tommy and her mother. By the hush she knew, without actually being able to hear, what they were talking about. She got up from the table and went to the door. She had been arguing both sides of the motorcycle incident in her mind, and she had decided that even though her father was probably right, she would have given Tommy the money. She didn't know why exactly, except that he wanted it, and she was used to giving him what he wanted. His requests were never unreasonable: help with his homework, extra change from her allowance because he had to pay for dates and she didn't. For his part he treated her as the most important girl in school and so in the eyes of others she was.

When Elise cracked open the kitchen door therefore, she was in sympathy with the scene she witnessed. Her mother was pulling a brown paper bag from a drawer and counting dollar bills into Tommy's hand. Tommy was then recounting them and tucking them into his pocket. After the transaction was completed, he kissed his mother on the cheek. It was at that moment Mrs. Ward looked up and saw Elise watching them. Her expression transformed. Her face tensed, and she frowned. Her hands darted up as though she needed to defend herself.

"What are you doing spying on us?" she declared.

"I'm not spying." Elise stepped into the kitchen.

"You were peeking through the door like a spy."

"Mother, I was just watching."

Tommy put his arm around his mother's narrow shoulders and gave them a squeeze. "It's okay, Ma. Lise won't tell."

Mrs. Ward's eyes darted to her son then back to her daughter. She attempted a smile, but Elise was staring at her confused now, and for a moment she looked as if she might cry. But then her expression hardened, and she drew herself up instead as though a rod had been inserted between her shoulders and her back. She moved into the kitchen and over to her mother. She took the brown bag from her mother's hands and scooped out the remaining fifty dollars or sixty dollars. "I guess the rest is mine," she said.

She met her mother's eyes, and the two of them stared at each other. They looked like mirror images at different junctures in time. They were both tight-jawed, their energy repressed in compact bodies which seemed at any moment ready to explode into some physical contact between them, but they didn't even touch. The older woman was greying, and for a moment the hardness in her face was softened by the suggestion of surprise around her eyes as if somewhere at a point she could no longer locate, her life had gotten away from her and taken a course of smaller expectations. The hardness in Elise's face was relieved by her youth and by the yearning in her eyes.

Tommy watched them. Their hostility, though suppressed, was far more threatening to the family than that between Tommy and his father. Neither of them was willing to face the breach, however, and Mrs. Ward wouldn't even admit its existence except as these occasional "flare-ups" as she called them. Though Tommy saw it, he wasn't one for baring wounds, and so he laughed now instead. "That's right, Lise, it's yours. Ma's saving it for your motorcycle."

Elise must have seen there was no use in pressing the point for she opened her hand and dropped the money back into the bag. "I just wanted to make sure."

Her mother blinked. She drew the bag to her. She had saved this money from her allowance. She saved every year secretly for emergencies and Christmas and, as it happened most years, for Tommy. Mr. Ward and the family knew of this secret cache, but they allowed her the secret and the security she took from $100-$150 stowed away in a kitchen drawer or closet shelf. Every year she changed the hiding place. Around February or March Elise would find the brown bag while searching for toilet paper or tin foil. She would unroll it, count the money, then roll it up again and leave it for her mother.

The breach between Elise and her mother was laid open the following summer, but not before the whole order of the family had broken apart. That summer the Wards were each busy in their own worlds. A new high school had opened, and Elise had been assigned to it and elected cheerleader for the coming year. She was attending cheerleading school and practice almost every day. Tommy had been accepted to the University of Tennessee and was commuting between Little Rock and Memphis in a round of pre-rush fraternity parties. Mrs. Ward was spending the summer canning fruits and entering roses into competition. And Joe Ward had taken the summer off from teaching to complete his master's thesis once and for all. The thesis was due when the university convened in September. (Actually it was past due for the deadline had already been extended twice.)

By August it became clear to Mr. Ward that he would not finish his thesis; he would not even come close for instead of working on the manuscript, he had gotten caught up in events leading to school opening that year. This was the year Little Rock was to integrate. Three years after the Supreme Court had declared school segregation uncon-stitutional in the South, the Little Rock School Board was instituting stage one of a desegregation plan. The first year's goal was modest: fifteen Negro students were to attend all-white Central High School. While other Southern cities had faced rioting and violence when they attempted the same, Little Rock didn't expect trouble. Little Rock was, in its own words, "a city of the new South." For his part Joe Ward had drafted an opinion piece for the *Gazette* supporting compli-ance; he'd attended meetings of concerned teachers, and he'd spent hours discussing the pros and cons of integration with anyone who wanted to listen.

The correlation between the impending desegregation at Central and Joe Ward's failure with his master's thesis was problematic, but it was the excuse he offered when he met with his advisor on a hot morning in mid-August. He had

journeyed to the university to ask for a further delay, at least
to the first of the year. If he bore down this fall, even with
the additional faculty meetings because of desegregation,
he thought he could finish. Ultimately he was aiming to get
a doctoral degree and to teach at the university. He had been
living with this dream ahead of him as long as he could
remember. His goal had been diffused by the daily demands
of high school history teaching—the quizzes and drills, the
advisorships to the history club, the newspaper, the debate
club. He advised more organizations than any other teacher
because more organizations asked him and appealed to his
vanity as one of the school's most popular teachers. Beyond
all the meetings and busy work, however, he still glimpsed
the larger idea he wanted to pursue. It related to the South
and American idealism. His advisor had told him the theme
was too broad for a master's thesis and had set Mr. Ward
writing instead on leadership differences between Grant and
Lee in several key battles. Not incidentally the topic paralleled
a book his advisor was working on at the time. He had
several of his students writing theses on Grant and Lee that
year. Joe Ward's greatest failure had been in not submitting
his thesis before his professor's own manuscript was due
at the publisher's.

Mr. Ward waited in Geoffrey Rawlin's office for almost
an hour before the grey-haired chairman of the history
department appeared. The morning sun blasted through the
closed windows heating the room to ninety-three degrees
according to the thermometer paperweight holding down
the single sheet of paper on the desk. The desk was a high-
polished mahogany as were the the Louis XV chairs in the
corner; the chairs matched the drapes which framed the
windows and the built-in book shelves. The office looked
like a study in one of the mansions on Edge Hill where
Geoffrey Rawlins lived. Margaret Randolph Rawlins, of the
tobacco-owning Randolphs, had decorated the office for her
husband, and the details, including a maroon leather desk
set, had her touch.

Dr. Rawlins entered the office swearing. He was holding up the edge of his seersucker suit jacket. "Goddamn taxi driver slammed the door on my coat, tore the damn pocket..." he declared. He took off the coat and examined the damage as he sat down at his desk. Dr. Rawlins didn't drive. He and his wife shared a chauffeur, and when she was using him, he relied on the less than dependable taxi service. "Goddamn drivers."

Dr. Rawlins pulled his appointments calendar to him and drew out a pair of reading glasses. He studied the calendar for a moment before he looked up. "Hotter than a whore's ass in here, Ward. Why didn't you open the windows?" Sweat was running down the sides of Mr. Ward's head; his face was flushed. He was smoking, and the glass and leather ashtray in front of him had accumulated a small mound of cigarette butts. "For Christ's sake take off your jacket."

Mr. Ward folded his navy suit jacket on the chair and loosened his tie. He allowed Dr. Rawlins to intimidate him because he'd never found an appropriate posture to assume with the man. Dr. Rawlins was a popular historian whose books Mr. Ward had read when he was in college. He disputed his teacher's most recent works for their unfounded judgments, but he had to admit the writing style flourished, and it was his style which kept Geoffrey Rawlins his readers and thus his publishing contracts.

"So, Ward, why are we here today? You have that thesis yet?"

"Almost..." Mr. Ward attempted a smile. "But I've been a little tied up, you know, with all this integration mess." He heard himself playing to Dr. Rawlins' sentiments already.

"Ah, so I read. You've been writing for the *Gazette* rather than for me." The old man smiled. "You don't really believe that prate you wrote, do you? To do less than obey the law is to betray ourselves and our forefathers. That's crap, Ward."

"I was referring to the Constitution's guarantee of..."

"Crap," Dr. Rawlins repeated mildly. "You haven't studied the facts of history. The Constitution was written by forty

102

white men, a third of whom owned slaves and whose descendants continued to own slaves almost a hundred years after the document was signed, sealed and delivered. I'm afraid you're distorting the facts of history to what you wish had happened. A fatal mistake for a historian."

Mr. Ward started to protest that he did no such thing. He preached to his students all the time that they had to go into history without opinions and judgment; he preached the point when it was irrelevant to the kind of factual recitation he taught in high school and was beyond the comprehension of most of his students. He could argue that this kind of judgmental history was the very crime Dr. Rawlins was guilty of in his latest books. But he said nothing. He was beginning to feel light-headed, and he needed Dr. Rawlins' good will right now. "If I could just have until Christmas, I'm sure I could finish," he said.

"Christmas!" Dr. Rawlins leaned forward in mock surprise. Actually he was starting to feel a little better sitting opposite this middle-aged student. At the moment Joe Ward looked particularly small and powerless. His shirt was drenched with sweat; his face was pained. He was feeling self-conscious about the odor he was starting to emit, and he was realizing that even if he got his extension, there was little chance he could finish by Christmas. By comparison Geoffrey Rawlins sat cooled in the breeze from the window he was blocking. Even in his early seventies, one year before retirement, five years after he was supposed to retire, he was in fit condition. "At the rate you're writing history, Ward, you'll be a part of it," he said.

"I think what I'm writing is important, sir," Mr. Ward offered.

"Important? Exactly what do you mean by important?"

"Original."

"Like your opinions in the *Gazette?*"

Mr. Ward didn't answer. He knew enough not to get into a debate with Geoffrey Rawlins over the integration of the South. But Dr. Rawlins persisted, "I have to admit it makes me wonder when a student of mine uses the Constitution

of the United States to justify the judicial branch's inter-
ference in a state's rights. It makes me wonder about his
understanding of the historical processes which formed this
nation and about his general overall aptitude as a historian."

"I think it's a question of interpretation, sir," Mr. Ward
said.

"That's your problem, Ward. Always has been. That's
why you can't finish your thesis. You think history is a matter
of opinion. History is history. The sooner you learn that,
the better." Dr. Rawlins picked up the calendar on his desk.
"How many extensions is that anyway?"

"This will make the third."

"I've never allowed a student three extensions. Why do
you think I should give you another?"

Mr. Ward sat forward on the straight-backed chair. He
unbuttoned the top button of his shirt and wiped his
forehead with a handkerchief. He pulled out another
cigarette. "Since I plan to go on for a doctorate, I view this
thesis as more than simply a paper," he answered. "I see
it as a place to work out my research techniques and overall
perspective."

"Bullshit," Dr. Rawlins said. He was still staring at his
appointments calendar, and his mind had jumped to his own
luncheon date with the dean and the case he was going to
make for his appointment as professor emeritus after he
retired this year.

"What?" Mr. Ward leaned even further forward on the
chair.

"Bullshit, I said." Dr. Rawlins began making notes on
a piece of paper for his arguments at lunch. He glanced up.
"Write the goddamn paper. You're not writing the Bible. But
as for a doctorate, I don't know where you're planning to
go, but..."

"I was thinking of the university."

Geoffrey Rawlins furrowed his eyebrows. "I'm afraid the
university accepts only a small, select group for its doctoral
program. Students who have clearly demonstrated they will
be the historians of the future." He paused and set the calen-

dar back in its place on the desk. His moist blue eyes rested on Mr. Ward. He drew out a handkerchief and wiped his eyes. Only his eyes gave away his age. They were rheumy and out of focus. He was too vain to wear the thickly-lensed glasses he needed; instead he wore his reading glasses and traveled in familiar territory — his home, the university, the country club. His life was so well-ordered that he could almost forget his handicap except occasionally when he was thrust into unfamiliar surroundings. That was what had happened this morning when the taxi driver let him off on the wrong corner. In his confusion Dr. Rawlins had tried to climb back into the cab just as it was pulling away, and he had fallen onto the curb and torn his jacket. It had taken him forty-five minutes of careful wandering to find his way to his office. As he looked at Joe Ward now, the memory of the morning passed through his mind, and his expression changed from one of impatience to pity towards this student who was lost in an unrealistic hope.

"You want my advice, Joe," he asked. It was the only time Mr. Ward could remember Dr. Rawlins calling him by his first name. "Finish your thesis; I'll give you the extension. Get your masters, get your pay raise and teach high school. It's a good job, a good life. Don't fool yourself." He stood up then. "Now I'm afraid I have a luncheon meeting I have to prepare for." He glanced about the room. "Do you see my fan anywhere?"

Mr. Ward shook his head without looking. He rose slowly from the chair. Had there been a mirror or had Dr. Rawlins been able to see more clearly, one of them might have noticed how unnaturally flushed Joe Ward had grown. But Dr. Rawlins patted him on the shoulder instead. "Take my advice, Joe. I've been around longer than you; I know what I'm talking about."

Mr. Ward nodded. He started down the corridor towards the stairs. Geoffrey Rawlins shouted over his head to his secretary. "Mary, where's my fan? Hotter 'n hell, and someone's stolen my goddamn fan!"

Mr. Ward left the red brick Humanities building and

headed across campus. It was almost ninety degrees and only 11:30; it was August 19, fifteen days before school opened. If he went away by himself with the thesis for the next two weeks, maybe he could get it moving again, he thought. He only had to write one hundred to one hundred and fifty pages. He had already written five times that much, but he had thrown most of it away. The problem was one of perspective. If he could only have an uninterrupted period to work out his perspective; yet he had given himself the time this summer. He had written page after page the first few weeks, but then he'd thrown the work away. It was prate, prattle, twaddle, as Dr. Rawlins would say. He was posturing what he thought Dr. Rawlins wanted to read, and he didn't believe the paper. When he wrote what he believed, he didn't trust his judgment enough to stand it against what by now had been published as Dr. Rawlins' view. He had let himself get intimidated by this man whose judgment he no longer respected but whose power seemed absolute. If Dr. Rawlins vetoed him for the doctoral program, he was out. Yet Joe Ward refused to think about that possibility. Dr. Rawlins would change his mind when he read his thesis, Mr. Ward told himself, for he still believed in the possibility of a vision that would elevate his work into the realm of original history.

As he moved towards the parking lot, his mind began to race over the facts of his paper towards that vision. Without realizing it, he was walking faster and faster until he was almost running. Hadn't Dr. Rawlins shown a genuine affection for him by the end of the interview today? The old man had just been in a cross humor; it was hot, so goddamn hot. Dr. Rawlins hadn't actually said he wouldn't be accepted. His opinion had been stated on a whim, in an aberrant moment because he was piqued by Mr. Ward's column in the *Gazette*. What Joe Ward didn't understand, however, though he sensed it in a corner of his being, was that once Geoffrey Rawlins made up his mind, it didn't matter what his initial reasoning had been; he stood behind his opinion as though it were doctrine. Mr. Ward also didn't understand that he could now turn in one hundred pages of nursery rhymes and get a master's for Dr. Rawlins had determined he would grant Mr. Ward the degree as compensation. He had decided on the spur of the moment too that more high school history teachers should get master's degrees—a topic and program he would discuss with the dean at lunch—and that Joe Ward would be his token teacher.

Mr. Ward was on the plaza between the Drama building and the parking lot when he fell. The sun had advanced overhead, and the heat reflected up from the pavement as well as down from the sun. Few people were about on campus. Those who were walked in the shade of the pine trees along the edge of the path. Under a spreading maple in the center of campus a boy and girl were sharing a picnic. Further away two secretaries strolled to the cafeteria carrying parasols over their heads. No one was in a hurry to get anywhere that day; there was nowhere to go for summer classes were over, and registration for fall hadn't yet begun.

At first no one noticed when Mr. Ward fell, at least no one came to his aid. But when he didn't get up, the boy rose from under the tree and walked over to him. "Too hot to be running, sir," he said as he bent down. Mr. Ward didn't move. The boy peered into his face which was now drained of color, and he called to his girlfriend. The girl stared at Mr. Ward for a moment. A slight breeze stirred the pine trees nearby. A hint of alarm rose in her voice as she said, "Maybe we should call an ambulance."

Mr. Ward was rushed to the nearest hospital and was admitted as having suffered a massive coronary. He remained in intensive care for three hours. Mrs. Ward arrived at the hospital around one, alone. She was not allowed to see her husband until 2:30 when it was determined he would not survive. She was rushed in to watch him take his last breaths. He died ten minutes later without regaining consciousness.

Mrs. Ward sat by herself for three hours in the hospital

waiting room. At the other end of the room were two women and a small child. The child was dressed in dirty white shorts and a pink halter. Periodically she would run to the peanut machine by Mrs. Ward then report back to her mother in a little girl's whisper how many peanuts she'd gotten. Every half hour a nurse came into the room and offered Mrs. Ward a styrofoam cup of coffee and suggested that she try her children again. Mrs. Ward had been unable to get in touch with Tommy or Elise, and she refused to go home alone. At one point one of the women had attempted a conversation with her, asking who she was waiting for. But Mrs. Ward's body grew rigid, and she answered with icy superiority, "We are not all waiting."

Finally at 5:45 she again pressed her coin into the pay phone, and this time Elise answered. "Come and get me," Mrs. Ward ordered.

"Where are you?"

She told her daughter she was at the hospital. She didn't explain why, and Elise didn't ask. Elise said instead, "I don't have the car."

"I have the car. You come and get me." Mrs. Ward's voice was angry as though Elise had failed her already.

When Elise arrived at the hospital, Mrs. Ward told her that her father was dead and that she had been waiting for three hours for someone to come for her. She straightened herself up in the chair and stared at Elise. Neither of them spoke. Elise squinted as if trying to take in what her mother had said. She drew her hand over her head and looked about the room: at the orange plastic chairs, the drinking fountain, the red peanut machine. The room was strange and unfamiliar and had no relation to her life. It was warm too, unbearably warm, and flooded with too much light.

"I told him he was pushing himself too hard," her mother argued. "And now he's dead." Mrs. Ward picked up her purse. She rose from the chair and started across the flecked linoleum towards the door. When she passed the two women and the child, she squared her shoulders as though her dignity were being appraised. At the door she turned and offered them an odd smile, then thrust herself outside.

Elise followed silently behind. Her mother strode across the parking lot to a green Plymouth and got in on the passenger's side. Elise opened the driver's door. She slid behind the wheel onto the worn olive green upholstery and waited for her mother to give her the keys. "He never listened to me," Mrs. Ward complained. "You and he were alike that way; you never listen to me."

Elise stared over the steering wheel. She wore a short pleated skirt and a white and orange blouse with an "H" on the back. Today had been the cheerleader's dress rehearsal for the first football game. She glanced at her mother, who was staring out the window at the floodlights in the parking lot. The sky was still bright, but it would grow dark soon. Elise didn't know what to say to her mother. She didn't ask for details; she didn't want the details for she didn't really believe her mother. Her father wouldn't die like this, without warning her. At that moment she suspected his death was simply another grievance for her mother to hold against her.

When they got home, Tommy was in the kitchen, bare-chested, drinking a beer. He'd already drunk several cans, and he looked around peevishly. "Where was everybody? Nobody's even made dinner." But seeing his mother's face, he stopped. "What's wrong?"

"Tommy, Tommy, Tommy...your father's gone." Mrs. Ward hurried to him. "He left us this morning without warning, and now he's gone."

Tommy looked over his mother's shoulder at Elise. "Dad's run off?" he asked. Elise was standing in the doorway, her body frozen in the white light of the fluorescent fixture on the ceiling. She stood at the edge of this room like a stranger. Her mother glanced at her now. She looked almost sorry as though she knew she were excluding her daughter but didn't know how else to act. The separation had been set too long before by emotions and feelings she couldn't even remember except that now they were a part of her. Perhaps she felt the way she did because her husband had always adored his daughter so or because Elise had come unplanned less than a year after Tommy, forcing her to give less time to her son. Or perhaps it was just her nature which bounded and constricted her love. She didn't reason through these possibilities; she simply felt a heightening of the loss as she saw Elise standing there.

"No, no," she answered Tommy instead. "He died, Tommy. This morning at the university. He had another attack only he didn't come back this time. I was going out to market, but I couldn't find the keys. Elise had put them on the chiffonier instead of the table, and I was looking for them when the phone rang. I thought it was you calling, but it was the hospital. If the keys had been where they were supposed to be, I wouldn't even have been here."

Mrs. Ward looked again at Elise, and it wasn't clear if she were blaming her or thanking her, and Elise wondered why her mother assumed she was the one who had misplaced the keys. "I would have been at the market and never would have known. I saw him just before he passed, but he didn't see me. He never saw me again."

She began to weep. Tommy put his other arm around her and sat her at the table. He let her cry on his shoulder as he rocked her back and forth in his arms. Elise watched them for a moment; then she left the room. In the hallway she stopped at the linen closet. From behind the wash cloths she drew forth a brown paper bag full of coins and dollar bills. She took the bag to her room where she hurled it through the window. As glass shattered around her, she let out a sob. It was the only sound she made as hundreds of coins flew out in all directions—shining silver and brass flashes of light suspended in the air, then pelting to the earth like a hard, unnurturing rain. She sank into the pink quilted chair by the window and looked out at the garden. She stared at the white rose bushes in last bloom. She didn't cry; she simply stared as the light faded and the night set in. And in her heart that night she took in part of the darkness.

THE BEGINNING OF VIOLENCE

Nashville, 1960

The wind shot through you that day like fate or some might say like the will of God. No matter what you did, it got you. It weaseled under the buttons of your coat, pulled off your scarf. You couldn't fight against it though you could stay indoors, but once you came out, you had to face the wind and find your way.

It was the day before Valentine's, and snow was falling in thick wet flakes, had been since early morning and threatened to keep on all afternoon. As I said, it was not a day to be outside, but I was. I was downtown on the arcade doing last minute shopping for a sorority party that night. We'd been decorating all morning, but we'd run out of crepe paper and balloons; and Janie, the food chairman, was afraid she'd run out of paper plates and cups so I said I'd go downtown and pick up everything.

I went to Woolworth's. At the Grand Ole Opry counter I bought a red plastic guitar set inside a big red plastic heart for the centerpiece on the officer's table. I was an officer. I was treasurer of the Kappa Alpha Thetas at Vanderbilt University.

I didn't feel like turning right around and going back into the cold so I stopped at the lunch counter for coffee and a grilled cheese sandwich. I was sitting there eating and reading "When Lilacs Last in the Door-Yard Bloom'd" for English class when a blast of air swept across my back. When I turned to see who was holding the door open, I saw dozens of Negroes coming into the store. They moved straight down the aisles then disappeared among the cheap jewelry and face powders and school supplies.

I turned back around and finished my sandwich and Whitman's poem. I was about to pay and leave when three Negroes sat down at the counter, one of them next to me. They all held brown paper bags with purchases they'd made. The girl beside me smiled, showing a curve of white teeth and asking more than most people thought she had a right to ask. I looked over my shoulder and saw thirty or forty more Negroes lining up to sit at the counter.

It took me a minute to understand what was happening. I'd grown up in Arkansas and Tennessee, and in nineteen years I'd never eaten beside a Negro. I'd never sat next to one on a bus or gone to the same bathroom. Things were changing in the South, but these were facts I'd lived with. Once in high school in Little Rock I'd signed a petition favoring integration, and that had almost gotten me thrown out of cheerleading. Some people thought anyone for the Negro was a Communist. I wasn't a Communist; I just thought the Negro should have a chance. And yet even feeling that way, I wasn't prepared to have the order of things put to question right where I was sitting.

The girl kept smiling. She had a soft mouth and big, dark eyes. Her hair was straightened, and she wore it like mine, in a pageboy with bangs. She was taller than me, and under her coat she looked strong. When she saw my poetry book on the counter, she reached into her pocket and took out a copy of the same book. I couldn't help but feel she'd just drawn her gun. I glanced away. My eyes fell on her hands; they were the color of dry soil, large and muscular and deeply lined like an old woman's.

I glanced at her friend next to her, but her friend's eyes were flat and hard, and her mouth looked set to tell me her mind. It was this girl who got me moving again. I'd been about to pay and leave when they'd sat down. My purse was open on the counter, and I went on counting out the change. I closed my wallet and purse; I gathered my bags, stood and left. The act of leaving wasn't a decision so much as a resumption of the way I was already going.

Not till I was outside in the blowing snow, moving towards the bus did I think about what I'd done, not till I was getting on the bus did I hear the words of the waitress: "I'm sorry, we don't serve coloreds here." All the way back to Vanderbilt, and as I walked on campus through what by now was a small scale blizzard, I kept thinking about those words. At the party that night, dancing under the crepe paper streamers we'd draped from the ceiling to make a tent, I could still hear the words and see the face of the girl.

The next morning I read about what had happened at Woolworth's on page ten of the *Nashville Tennessean*. Without knowing it, I'd been in the middle of Nashville's first sit-in. I decided to write my own version of what I'd seen, and I turned it into the college paper. The paper ran the story under the headline: "At the Counter: A Student's View." The editor asked me to write on what happened next though no one knew what was going to happen next, but the editor thought something would. He told me I should stress the Vanderbilt angle. I wasn't sure what the Vanderbilt angle was, but that's the way I got involved. Before the year was over, I'd witnessed more than a dozen sit-ins.

The next time I saw the girl was two weeks later. In between the snow had kept falling, making it one of the worst winters in Nashville's history. During those days on the front pages of the *Tennessean*, Jack Parr was battling NBC over his contract with the Tonight Show while in Washington Lyndon Johnson battled for national civil rights legislation. A hundred miles away in Chattanooga fighting had broken out after sit-ins there. The Nashville sit-ins had stepped up but were still reported on the inside pages. So far no arrests had been made.

All week rumors had been going around that the largest sit-in ever would take place downtown Saturday. I decided to go. Jeff, my boyfriend, tried to argue me out of it then said he'd go with me, but he got sick after a fraternity party Friday night, and so I went by myself. No one at the sorority house could believe I would go, but I did.

When I got there, thousands of people were already on the arcade, and policemen lined the streets. Just after noon the first demonstrators showed up, including the girl. She was wearing the same oversized brown coat; on her head she wore a white crocheted cap. She walked with her head down, bowed against the wind. She didn't look at anyone. Most of the protesters were students, and they were glancing around at the crowds on the sidewalk. But she stared straight ahead. She was so focused that she didn't even answer her friend who spoke to her as they entered McClellan's Variety Store.

I followed them inside. The lunch area was packed with people standing about waiting to see what would happen. The girl made her way through the crowd to a seat at the counter. One by one other students took stools under the faded pictures of salisbury steak, Irish stew, hamburger deluxe. A railing separated the eating area from the rest of the store, and the press stood behind it among hair nets and hair rollers; I took my place with the press.

A waitress approached the girl. "I'm sorry; we don't serve coloreds here," she said. "You'll have to leave."

"A cup of coffee, please," the girl answered.

"I'm sorry, we don't serve coloreds," the waitress repeated.

"A cup of coffee."

Half a dozen white teenagers stepped into the area and started catcalling. They picked out a white demonstrator sitting near the girl. "Nigger lover! Nigger lover!" they taunted. A man with a cigar began blowing smoke into the face of the girl and the other students. Several more teenagers moved in, bumping against the protesters, trying to knock them off their stools.

The students didn't react. The girl pulled her poetry book from her pocket and opened it on the counter. She was starting to read when suddenly she let out a cry. I looked and saw a teenager squash his lighted cigarette on her back. I couldn't tell if he'd actually burned her or only ruined her coat. She jerked around. She stared straight at the boy. She

114

met his jeer with a question which again asked more than people were willing to have asked of them. Her look must have shaken him or touched something in him because he stepped away. His friends started lighting their cigarettes and pressing them out on the backs of other students, but the boy left the store. The exchange took only a moment, but in it I saw some possibility, some viewpoint I hadn't considered before.

Before I could think about exactly what this was, however, someone shoved a white protester from his stool and began hitting him in the ribs. The man blowing cigar smoke laid a fist into the back of a black student. Other teenagers began pulling at the hair of the girls sitting at the counter. None of the demonstrators raised a hand to defend himself. I saw in the faces of many, anger and a struggle not to fight back. But in the face of the girl I saw something else.

The police finally arrived, but only after the teenagers had run away. They told the protesters they had to leave because the store management had decided to mop the floor. When they refused, the police moved in, taking hold of the students one by one and escorting them into police vans waiting outside. The girl was arrested.

I followed the rest of the day's events, including the beatings of several Negroes late in the afternoon at Woolworth's where no police were around. Members of the press, including me, watched as a white teenager pulled a Negro protester from a chair and hit him again and again in the face spreading open his nose with a fist, bloodying both their skins with the same blood and as another white pushed a Negro student down a flight of stairs, sending his arms and legs clattering against the metal. None of the experienced press stepped in to stop what was happening; instead they stood recording the incidents so I did the same. Yet inside I was trembling as if someone had hit me, and I wanted to strike back. I didn't know what to do with the violence I suddenly felt. I left the store.

I decided to meet the girl. I told the newspaper editor I wanted to write a profile of a demonstrator, and he agreed.

I found out her name was Cynthia Davis. She was a senior at Fisk University. When I called her, she at first refused to be interviewed, said there were better people than herself, but I convinced her she was the one I wanted to talk to. She agreed to meet me at a diner near Fisk after classes Friday.

Fisk is only a few miles from Vanderbilt, but like most everyone else, I'd never been in the neighborhood let alone seen the campus. The streets around it were quiet and lined with trees and houses. The campus itself was much smaller than Vanderbilt's and more run-down. It had one main walkway. On both sides of the walk were dorms and class-rooms. I decided to go in just to look. I stayed only long enough to walk to the end of the path and back again, but in that time the world closed in around me. I was the only white person, at least the only one I saw, and I felt every-one staring at me.

When I reached the end of the walk, I read the sign in front of a huge Victorian Gothic building. I tried to concen-trate on the fact that this was the first building of the univer-sity, the first in the country built to educate Negroes, but the truth is I was thinking only about myself and the color of my skin for all at once my skin seemed alive as if it were plugged in and glowing and separate from me. For a minute I couldn't feel myself under it. To be suddenly separate from your body is scary. Everyone thinks you're your body because that's what they see only you know you're not. I've heard of people coming back after dying, saying they've watched themselves from outside, watched everyone else watching their bodies while they knew that wasn't them only they couldn't make themselves heard. I don't want to go on too much, but that's what I felt: a separation I couldn't make my way across. The space between me and my skin was like the space between me and the Negroes, and in it was a kind of panic and darkness I wanted to strike out against. For the first time I understood why separation was the beginning of violence.

I hurried back to the car I'd borrowed. I locked the doors and sat for a moment. Finally I started the engine and drove to the diner a few blocks away.

It was five o'clock, and only a handful of students were at the counter and in the booths. When I came in, they glanced up, and again I felt my skin starting to glow. Behind the counter the waitress stared at me. She had a thick ridge of brown hair and dull eyes. She was wiping the stained formica with a rag which she tossed in the sink behind her without taking her eyes off me.

At first I didn't see Cynthia in any of the tall wooden booths. From the front of the restaurant I could see only the person sitting at the edge of the booth facing forward. But then on the hook of the last booth I spotted the rough brown coat. When I approached, I expected her to recognize me as the girl she'd sat beside in Woolworth's, but instead I realized she too saw me only as the singular white person in the diner.

She was studying at the table. She wore a grey knit sweater and a white crocheted cap on her head. I'd never seen her without her coat. She was much thinner than I expected. Her shoulders were narrow and her neck quite slender. Again I noticed her hands; they seemed disproportionately large now.

"Cynthia Davis?" I asked.

She nodded.

I sat down and moved towards the wall. Immediately I was hidden from view of the other people. "Thank you for meeting with me." She didn't answer. I glanced at her books on the table, and tried to think of what to say. "Do you study here often?"

She nodded again, watching me without speaking. She didn't seem hostile, only reserved. I'd wanted to meet her to find out where she came from and how she'd arrived at this point in her life. Yet as she stared at me without recognition, I realized I'd also come here to have her meet me and approve of me, and her failure to recognize my imperative made me falter.

I set right into the interview. I asked about her family. She was third in a family of six children from Fayette County,

Tennessee. Her father was a preacher, a small plot farmer and owner of a modest dry goods store. Her mother worked the farm and raised the children. Cynthia would be the first of her family to graduate from college. At Fisk on a scholarship, she was an A-student, an English major, and she hoped to go on to law school next year.

She answered my questions without self-consciousness, and because she was at ease with herself, I began to feel more at ease. When I'd run through all the facts I wanted to know, I set my pad and pencil down. Leaning forward on the table, I fixed my eyes on the translucent lobes of her ears which supported the weight of heavy metal hoops. I stared at these as I tried to form the question I had come to pose. Finally I asked, "Why don't you fight back? The other day, when that boy burned you, why did you just sit there?"

"He was bigger than me," she answered.

I frowned.

"What would it have proved?"

"That he can't get away with what he did."

She smiled. "But he can. We both know that. Fighting him wouldn't have changed anything."

"How does getting beaten up or burned change anything?"

"It doesn't." She picked up a napkin from the table. She was quiet for a moment; then she asked. "You ever taken a hound dog hunting?" I smiled, surprised by the question. "When a hound dog gets a scent, he won't let go. He doesn't care if it's raining or it's getting dark or it's time to go home to bed. You can beat him; you can pull his collar till you choke him, but if he's got the scent, he'll do everything he can to take it to the end. Our movement's like that hound dog. We got the scent, and no one can beat it out of us or burn it out of us. The only thing they can do is show their own meanness."

She began folding the napkin in her broad hands. Her expression was serious, yet the corners of her mouth turned up, almost smiling, as though she were extending tolerance not only to me but to herself. "We used to think the white man controlled our lives," she said, "only since we can't control the white man, we thought we had no control. But it doesn't matter what white people say we are; it doesn't matter what unjust laws say we have to do. We know who we are. First and foremost we are God's children, and no one can turn us into hateful, beaten-down human beings; no one has that power. Power—that's the scent. It comes from treating a man right. Once you understand that, it will change your life. Jesus Christ showed us how. Mahatma Ghandi showed the people of India they could do the same thing."

As she spoke, her curious smile remained as if she understood the difficulty of her point of view. She spoke deliberately. She wasn't carried away by her words but reasoned through to her conclusions with a logic as careful as any lawyer's. "The righteousness of our cause will win over the hearts of good men and women and eventually change a whole system," she insisted. She glanced down at the napkin which she'd shredded into a small mound of confetti. She swept the paper into the palm of her hand and dumped it in the ashtray.

"From what I've observed," I offered cautiously, "your friends aren't as free of the hate and anger as you. Perhaps you understand more."

Her shoulders straightened against the back of the booth; her face roused. "Don't try to separate us," she warned. "You can't choose among us. What I understand, we all understand."

"I don't think that's true. Your friend next to you, both times I saw her, she was angry. She wanted to strike back; I saw it in her face. You didn't. I understand what I saw in her; I don't understand what I saw in you."

"I'm angry. Anyone not angry is asleep. But we have to struggle with our own weaknesses as well as with society's."

"But if your movement depends on society having a conscience and that conscience stirring...well, frankly, I doubt how many good-hearted men and women you're going to find."

"Then that doubt is your weakness, isn't it?" she offered.

I looked up. She stared at me with a calm, penetrating gaze which struck at that separation I'd felt on campus, first from myself then from others. I didn't answer. Instead I began asking about her friends, again setting her apart from them. Again she held to the group, answering only in the plural. She emphasized she was committed to the *Christian* ethic of nonviolence for only as one was able to yield himself to God's goodness was he able to express his own and see goodness in others. Yet as we talked now, I felt uneasy for she'd seen something in me which I hadn't seen, yet which, when named, I knew: a doubt, a smallness of belief, a smallness of heart. I had wanted her to know me, but now I resented what she'd chosen to know. I found myself wanting to expose something in her.

We talked almost an hour as the diner started to fill with students. One by one the booths around us sounded with chatter. Cynthia was leaning closer to me so we could hear each other, her head propped between her ashen palms, her sweater pushed up above rough elbows. Finally as the interview wound down, circling around questions I'd already asked, the quick light in her eyes resumed a quieter glow and her half smile drew back into the reserved lines of a stranger's.

I wrote my article for the paper the next week. It brought me immediate attention. I didn't exactly glorify Cynthia Davis, but I set her up as an example of a generation of blacks with expectations to achieve beyond their parents and with a commitment to American ideals of equality. In writing it, I forgot for the moment my own discomfort over what she'd seen in me, and I wrote in an inflated prose that would touch the sentimental strain in a white, liberal audience. I also told the story of a girl's ambitions which would offend those of a different persuasion. In the article I mentioned only that Cynthia's family lived in Fayette County.

The next week a reporter for the *Nashville Tennessean* called me to ask if the *Tennessean* could run my story as a side piece with a larger article they were doing on inter-college contact in the civil rights movement. The reporter was particularly interested in the fact that I'd gone over to Fisk to have the interview. I agreed. It would be my first paid article. Because the audience of the *Tennessean* was statewide, the editor wanted to know exactly where Cynthia's family lived, and so I gave him the town's name just outside of Memphis, and he printed it.

I thought of calling Cynthia and telling her about the story, but I didn't. I suppose I was afraid she'd object. I was also in the middle of mid-terms. I finally did call her Sunday, the day the article appeared. I phoned that afternoon, but she wasn't in. I left a message for her to call me back and then forgot about her. For the next few days friends and people I hardly knew stopped to talk about the story. They didn't talk so much about what it said as the fact I'd had it published in the *Tennessean*. Finally on Wednesday when I hadn't heard from Cynthia, I called again, and this time a friend of hers got on the phone.

"Cynthia's not here," she said. The friend's voice was strained, but matter-of-fact. "Her father's store was bombed Sunday night. Her brother's in the hospital. I don't know when she'll be back." Her friend didn't say anything about the article. I didn't know if she or Cynthia had even seen the article. I couldn't be sure the bombing was a result of the article.

I didn't see Cynthia Davis again. I phoned her several times, but she was never there. Then school got busy. I was starting to write freelance for the *Tennessean*, and I quit calling. At one of the sit-ins that spring I saw her friend, whom I recognized from that first day at Woolworth's, and I went over to her. She answered my questions formally. She told me Cynthia had taken a leave from Fisk to help at home and in the store until her brother got out of the hospital. She told me nobody knew how long that would be or how her brother would adjust for among his injuries, his right hand had been blown off.

The Nashville sit-ins kept on through the spring. There

were more arrests, more beatings of Negroes, negotiations with white business and political leaders, a cessation of arrests and sit-ins during negotiations, an economic boycott of downtown stores, a bombing of a black lawyer's home. But finally on May 10, less than three months after the first sit-in, an agreement was announced. Six downtown lunch counters would open on an "unbiased basis." The victory was the first of many to follow in Nashville. In the annals of southern history in the early 1960s, the Nashville movement was considered a nonviolent success story. Cynthia Davis was not among the names who moved onto prominence out of that movement. To my knowledge, she never returned to Fisk.

I've thought about Cynthia Davis from time to time since then. Once the following fall on the way back to school, I drove through Memphis with the intention of going to see her, but I lost courage. To be honest, I didn't want an answer. If there was an answer. I didn't want to be told that what happened was my fault. In some ways I was sure it was; and yet in others, no matter what anyone said, I wouldn't accept the blame. I didn't know what to do with it, and I didn't see how having it helped anyone.

I changed because of what happened in small, slow ways. By the spring of my junior year, I'd dropped out of my sorority. I became wary of my own ambition. I began to regard it as a subtle, unpredictable beast which, if I was not alert, would bite with sharp teeth.

When I think about what happened now, I account it to the wind. To what happens because of all that's happened before for reasons you don't understand because you're in the middle of them and because you don't understand yourself. I don't account it to fate or the will of God or any other cosmic design. I account it to my ignorance of design. And as I said, to the wind. I let the flow take me with it because I hadn't learned to face the wind, to pick up the scent but not be blown about. Because I didn't heed dark, unexposed places in myself, I fell inside one of them and perhaps took another with me.

M

DEATH STALKS A BUILDING ONCE IT ENTERS

r. Isaacs stood on the edge of the circle of women, his small grey eyes blinking at the sun. As he listened to their talk, his own lips moved, making no sound but warming up to the words. He began rubbing his hand back and forth over the fine brush cut of his white hair. Finally he eased closer to the group. "I didn't know..." he said. "It upsets me..." he tried again. "How is one to know..." he stammered trying to say how he felt, but the women talked anxiously without him. He wiped the back of his hand across his face; from his nose protruded small white hairs. He began to finger the air at his sides. He had been a furniture maker twenty-five years ago, and when he grew nervous, his fingers worked over cabinets and tables in his mind.

From the park a brisk autumn wind gusted and kicked up scraps of paper and dirt at Mr. Isaacs' feet, swelled his jacket and pants about him like the shell of a heartier self. He darted around then paused. From his building emerged a willowy, dark-haired woman. He stopped to watch her. She stood in the doorway looking up at the sun. The way she held her head, cocked to one side, the way she stood, feet apart, uncertain in their course made Mr. Isaacs stare. She wore tight pants and a loose high-fashioned jacket. As Mr. Isaacs watched her, he noticed the round beginnings of her belly expecting a child. Quickly he shuffled towards her. "Did you hear?" he called.

She looked at him, and her face softened: "Good afternoon."

"Did you hear?" He pursued, his voice urgent now. "The widow on the sixth floor, she died. She went out shopping, and then she came home, and then she died." His fingers began rummaging through the air. His eyes searched the young woman's face.

"I saw an ambulance," she offered, "coming home from work this morning."

"The widow just died," Mr. Isaacs repeated. "Nobody knew—if she even knew, I do not know—but she died." The girl's mouth set in a tight line, and she drew full attention on Mr. Isaacs. "I myself did not know the widow," he hastened to explain. "I was in her apartment only once. I thought you knew her. I thought you lived on the sixth floor and knew her."

"I live on your floor," she said. "We're neighbors."

"Oh." Mr. Isaacs stared at her then shook his head. His fingers moved faster against the wind. "Well, it upsets me, you know." He continued to stare into her face. Her skin was smooth, olive—young skin; her thin mouth wore a touch of pink. "How is one to know..." He dropped his eyes. "I thought you knew her."

From the circle of women, a grey-haired lady broke away and hastened towards Mr. Isaacs. Her hair flared in all directions, free in the wind. "Mr. Isaacs!" she called, waving her hand. "What is it you are doing? You broadcasting this over the neighborhood? If death is to be broadcast, let the television broadcast it." Mrs. Isaacs shook her head at her husband then looked kindly towards the young woman. "Why are you telling this girl? She is young. She don't have to worry." Mrs. Isaacs' face began to twitch above her eye, and her hand darted to the spot. Her fingers were knotted and thin as her husband's.

"I did see an ambulance," the girl repeated.

Something in her face made Mr. Isaacs want to reach out and touch her. Behind the large, determined eyes, a flicker...a passing of fear or sadness...something. Mr. Isaacs looked at her apologetically. "I thought she lived on

124

the sixth floor," he told his wife. "I thought she knew the widow."

"Solomon, she is next door to us. She is the model for the magazines. She is the one with the handsome husband —such an important man he looks in his suit."

Mr. Isaacs stared again at the young woman. He nodded, smiling now. "Ah...your husband, he invited us to visit in your apartment one day. Such fine furniture—mahogany, rosewood—such fine pieces of furniture to have so young."

Mrs. Isaacs nodded. "And her husband...to have such a handsome husband." Mrs. Isaacs reached out and touched the girl. "You are young," she said, glancing at the girl's rounding belly. "It is not for you to worry."

The young woman drew her brightly-colored jacket around her. As her hand passed over her belly, it paused, and the fear Mr. Isaacs had seen returned to her eyes. She nodded to the couple; then she moved off towards the park filled with the rust and orange leaves of the long Indian summer. Turning in the other direction, Mr. and Mrs. Isaacs walked to the corner to catch the half-fare bus to the supermarket.

When Mrs. Isaacs awoke from her afternoon nap, her husband was gone. The two of them had lain down as usual on the pink bedspread after they returned from shopping. But when Mrs. Isaacs reached out her hand, she touched only empty space beside her. She lay there listening. Sometimes Mr. Isaacs rose first and fussed in the kitchen with dinner. But she heard only the whirring of the humidifier in the corner. Quickly she slipped on her carpet slippers. As she hurried towards the living room, her throat began to close.

Once before Mr. Isaacs had run away. It was ten years ago, after Eddie Rawlins died. She still remembered the silences. Like death, the silences. Five days he was gone until the police finally brought him home tattered and worn, found him sleeping on a park bench. It wasn't from her he had run, he explained meekly; it was to think, to figure out

125

the rest of his life, to figure if he wanted the rest of his life. "So it is for us all, Solomon," she had said. "But it is life we got to choose."

Mrs. Isaacs hurried now out of the apartment. Her eyes darted around the hallway—pea green walls, chipped molding, cracked tiles. It was an old building as many of the tenants were old though already on the first floor the new owners were laying tiles and papering the walls with flowers. Young people were beginning to move into the empty apartments. Everyone should buy their apartment; that is what the new owners said, but they themselves had no money to buy. Her husband's friends had left long ago —died or moved into nursing homes. Her husband had to spend his time with the women, and Mrs. Isaacs knew he was not happy.

Quickly she moved next door. She rang the buzzer. She planned what she would say. She would say: I thought my husband perhaps stopped by to say hello. She would keep her voice calm so as not to cause alarm. The door opened a crack. Mrs. Isaacs' face began to twitch. "Hello..." she ventured. The young woman opened the door further. Her hair hung tangled on her shoulders; her eyes were red; her whole face was distorted from crying. Mrs. Isaacs stared. Quickly the girl tried to straighten her hair.

"I am sorry to bother you at this hour," Mrs. Isaacs began, averting her eyes, "but my husband...I thought my husband, Mr. Isaacs, by a chance might have stopped to visit you."

The girl stared down at the diminutive woman. "He was coming to visit me?" she asked.

"That is what I don't know," Mrs. Isaacs said. The young woman watched her, and Mrs. Isaacs was surprised by her attention. "It is nothing," she added hastily. "I thought only that he might be here. He liked talking to you...this afternoon when he talked to you." She looked away. The girl had seen her fear. "I am sorry I have bothered you."

Opening the door wider, the girl motioned for her to come inside. "You're not bothering me. I'm sorry, I haven't seen your husband." Her voice wavered.

"It is not for you to worry," Mrs. Isaacs insisted. "He slipped to the store perhaps. The old man forgets to tell me." The girl nodded, allowing her the lie. Mrs. Isaacs stared up into her finely featured face, swollen by the tears. Why was one this young so sad? When the girl saw her watching, she tried to smile, but Mrs. Isaacs would not release her from the question.

The girl retreated into the apartment. At a mirror in the hallway she picked up a brush and began pushing it through the long strands of her hair. She concentrated on brushing as if it would restore order.

Slowly Mrs. Isaacs followed inside. The rooms were dark, cold. The shades were drawn, and only thin strips of sunlight filtered through. Mrs. Isaacs stood behind the girl and watched her. At last the young woman lifted her eyes and steadied them on Mrs. Isaacs. She shrugged her shoulders as if apologizing to the older woman. "I get depressed sometimes," she said, "over the baby. I want to be..." She hesitated. "People say I could be...I'm only twenty." Her voice faltered. "I could be somebody..."

Mrs. Isaacs stared at her. On the table she saw a tall glass half-filled with Epsom salts and an open bottle of whiskey. She shuddered. Such a drink would make the girl vomit uncontrollably. Was she trying to hurt the baby? "Is a baby a thing to depress?" she asked. "It is a thing to make happy." Her voice insisted. "A new life...how lucky to give new life." The two women stared at each other, and the silence separated them. The girl turned away. "To punish yourself, to punish the baby—it's not right," Mrs. Isaacs declared.

"My husband..." the girl said nervously, "...he'll be home soon." She brushed her hair harder.

Mrs. Isaacs turned towards the living room. On the wall light shifted through the blinds, and on the floor she saw a blanket. The huddled shape of the cover told her this was where the girl had been lying, curled up in the afternoon, crying alone, fighting off darkness as the room grew cold around her.

"Your husband, he does not know you lie here and cry because you are to have a baby?" Mrs. Isaacs asked. The girl pushed the brush more determinedly; she didn't answer. "A husband should know such things," Mrs. Isaacs said. "He should know how a wife feels." She watched the girl. "And a wife," she added, "should know how a husband feels."

The girl looked in the mirror at the image of herself and the old woman silhouetted against the dusk. Mrs. Isaacs' skin stretched tightly over the small bones of her face, and the wrinkles seemed carved into her skin. Her eyes were fixed on the bottle of Epsom salts...the smoky brown jar... 'cathartic use '... 'Keep Out of Children's Reach.' Suddenly the old woman's hand darted up and swept the jar to the floor, sending glass shattering and salt spewing in all directions.

"Ah-h-h!" the girl jumped back. She turned, set to rebuke Mrs. Isaacs, but she saw behind the old woman's eyes a frantic light.

"Now to excuse me," Mrs. Isaacs insisted, "I must go find Mr. Isaacs." A chill passed through the old woman's body. She pushed her way towards the door. In that bottle she had seen death...seen it poured into the girl to kill the child. Death stalked a building once it entered. Quickly she must find her husband.

The girl stood without moving, then suddenly frightened, she rushed after the woman. "I'll help you look," she declared.

Together the two women left the apartment.

It was the young woman who suggested they look on the sixth floor. When they got out of the elevator, they heard a tapping sound, the slow rap...rap...rap of a hammer. The sound filled the hallway, echoing off the walls like the sluggish tick of a metronome. The noise came from the half-opened door of Apartment 6B.

"That is where the widow lived," Mrs. Isaacs said. She backed away from the door. "I do not want to go where death has been." She stiffened her back against the wall.

128

The girl eased over towards the apartment. "Hello?" she called from the hallway. She pushed the door open. "Hello?" she called again.

A voice answered, "Who is it calling?"

Slowly the young woman moved inside. The apartment itself looked dead: cracked brown wallpaper, faded rose-flowered drapes, worn carpet matting on the floor. From the living room a thin beam of light shone and drew the girl towards it. In its shadows she could see shapes—pieces of furniture upturned and stacked in the middle of the room. In the midst of the furniture, she saw a man. In his hands he held tacks and nails and a hammer. He looked up at her, and his lips began fluttering as though unhinged, forming words to himself.

"Mr. Isaacs," she whispered. His face was pale, and his eyes seemed lost in their sockets. He muttered to himself. "Mr. Isaacs," the girl declared.

He stared at her. Slowly his face filled with recognition, and he grinned. "Ah, you are Mrs. Ryan from next door to me," he said. "You have come to see the widow? I am sorry," his face grew solemn, "she died this morning." He banged on a chair. "I am fixing her furniture. Such fine furniture. The superintendent said I could fix it for her children. In case they come, they will want the furniture."

"Yes..." said the girl uneasily. She looked around at the three stick chairs, two tables, a stool: secondhand maple pieces, the kind brought off the streets or found in cheap motel rooms. On the broken stool sat a lamp. By its stream of yellow light Mr. Isaacs rapped his hammer on the bottom of a chair. The whole room seemed to shrink around this light and focus on Mr. Isaacs as if the room now possessed him. Tap...tap...tap. He hit against the furniture, missing the nails but banging still.

"It is for the children..." he told the girl again. He motioned for her to come closer.

Slowly the young woman moved towards him. The smell of medicine was thick in her nose and throat. She kept her eyes fixed on Mr. Isaacs. His face was pinched up around

129

his mouth where he held the tacks between his teeth. And he hammered...hammered against the silence.

"Your wife..." the girl whispered, "your wife is waiting." "I must work here." Mr. Isaacs smiled. "You understand I must stay." His hand reached out and touched her.

She drew back. The chill of his body passed into her. "Your wife," she pleaded. Suddenly he frightened her. The whole room frightened her. "Please come." She backed toward the door. She didn't belong in this room.

"I must stay," he insisted, "I..." Mr. Isaacs looked up to speak, but then he stopped. In the doorway stood his wife. Her thin hands clasped her skirt, and she stared down at him. "Esther!" he called. "I have been asked to fix the furniture for the widow's children. I must stay."

Mrs. Isaacs' face was drained of color. "Solomon," her voice rasped, "the widow has no children." Her words were barely audible. "You must come."

"But, Esther, I will be making us some money now. I will buy you a hat. In a new hat, you are the prettiest woman I ever saw."

"Solomon," her voice suddenly broke through. "Solomon," she cried out, "you must come!" Her eyes drew wide, and her hands held the door molding.

Mr. Isaacs shrank from her, hunched his shoulders against the table, defended himself from her words. His expression grew distant and his lips started smacking his own silent, formless sounds.

"Solomon!" Mrs. Isaacs wailed.

All at once the girl darted into the living room. She grabbed the old man's arms, began wrestling him from the floor. She tried lifting him by the armpits, struggled to free him from the furniture cage about him. His body felt cold and rigid as it fought her, but she pressed him to her warmth, pressed the warmth to herself and fought to free them both from this room. "You must come..." she begged.

In the doorway Mrs. Isaacs stared horrified. "You *must* come," she demanded. "You must not accept, Solomon. I do not accept. Always we must fight!"

Mr. Isaacs pulled back. The girl, his wife...their faces confused him. They saw something in the room with him he did not see. "Esther...Esther..." he tried to soothe, but her face would not relent. "Mrs. Ryan..." he pleaded, but the young woman continued to pull him. He let his body go limp, resisted the girl by giving her no force to fight against, but still she dragged him. Her face strained with his weight.

Finally, seeing the girl's pain, Mr. Isaacs gave in. He stood upright, and reluctantly he followed. At the door he took his wife's hand. "Esther..." he said, trying now to comfort her. "A fine new life is coming to our building, eh, Esther?" He looked over at the girl's belly and grinned. But his wife did not answer, and the girl did not smile.

At the elevator the young woman watched the couple. Mr. Isaacs' face was placid now, but Mrs. Isaacs' had filled with worry, and she held tightly to her husband's hand.

"Tonight..." the young woman said hastily, "...tonight you must come and visit with us. My husband and I would like to have you visit."

Mrs. Isaacs turned to the girl. For a moment they stared at each other. And then Mrs. Isaacs nodded. "If it is what you want," she said, "then we will come."

THE IMPOSTOR

Harry Brown read the funeral notice in the newspaper for the third time. Sitting at the table in his kitchen, he stirred his cereal and calculated the best route to the mortuary. Highway 202 to Bernardsville to Mt. Airy Road or perhaps Highway 287 straight to Mt. Airy Road.

The Weiner funeral would be his fourth in two months. There had been the Mooney funeral, then the Jamison, and two weeks ago, the Josephs. After the Jamison's funeral, Harry had decided to go only to Jewish funerals. He was part Jewish himself, and even though his wife had been Episcopalian and his children had been raised Episcopalian, he'd decided a Jewish widow would make him the best wife.

Harry reached over and added another spoonful of sugar to his cereal. When Sara was alive, she used to cook him full breakfasts of eggs and bacon and toast even though he was never hungry in the morning. Now he ate cornflakes. He sipped his coffee and lingered at the table. A clear autumn day shone through the open back door. The sky was cloudless, and a breeze rustled the wind chimes in the yard. Through the screen he could see the maple trees already turning red and yellow. Perhaps today would be the day he found himself a wife. He put on his glasses and again read the notice:

Abraham Weiner, 66. Partner in Weiner and Kroll, Accts. Beloved husband of Sadie. Devoted father of Rebecca. Services 10 a.m. Thursday, October 6. Somerset Memorial Park, Basking Ridge.

Before Sara had died, she had told him to get married again. "You need a woman, Harry, to look after you," she had said. He wondered if she had a woman in mind, but she had died before he could ask. That was almost two years ago. Only in the last few months had he decided to find a wife.

At first after Sara died, he wouldn't think of another woman. His children had tried to look after him then, especially his daughter-in-law Susie. Susie used to bring by two and three meals a week in tupperware bowls which she would store in his freezer—spaghetti casserole in pink tupperware, macaroni and cheese in yellow, and meatloaf in blue. Susie catalogued all the meals according to color on a sheet of paper. The first few weeks he hadn't eaten Susie's food, but then his freezer started to overflow with little blue and green and yellow plastic bowls, and finally he began to eat just so she would take home the bowls. Susie wasn't a very good cook. She cooked like Sara, thick starchy meals he had never liked.

At least Susie tried though. His other daughter-in-law Laura, who was a better cook, came by only twice that first month with hastily picked flowers from her garden. She spent the whole time talking about how busy she was in the community theatre. Laura had a flair for the dramatic, and in a way he enjoyed her company more than Susie's, but she was so full of herself, she allowed little space for him.

It was his son Dick who had first mentioned that he should start thinking about getting married again. The thought had occurred to him too, but he had hidden from it as he would from a naked woman in his closet. He had thought his children would think him disloyal, and he wasn't sure Sara really meant what she said. Then one afternoon Laura drove up waving an invitation at him. She'd gotten him invited to a bridge tournament at one of the better clubs in town. "You're still a handsome man, Harry," she told him. "You've got to give women a chance to meet you." She breezed in, dropped off the invitation then hurried out again, but after she left, he'd felt excited.

That night Harry studied himself in the mirror. He wasn't bad looking at that. He was only sixty-seven, recently retired. He still had his hair, at least a grey-brown ridge which sprouted around the base of his scalp like a fallen crown. He had a slight paunch, but who hadn't? His skin was good too, and with the tan he'd gotten from gardening, he looked almost distinguished, he thought.

The next evening Harry dressed carefully for the tournament. He wore his brown suit, the one with the thin orange stripe through it, his brown and white checked tie and his brown fedora hat. He dressed to look respectable, but also like a man with a little dash. Without even trying that night, he received two invitations for dinner the following week. At each he was to make up the fourth for bridge with three widows.

At first Harry didn't admit to himself he was looking for a wife. He was simply "going out." But one afternoon after months of playing bridge in strange widows' living rooms, Susie asked if he'd met any "nice" women, and he had to admit to himself that he had met no one he would consider for a wife. The problem with meeting women this way was that there were always so many of them and they were all so eager that the search was no fun.

Then one morning two months ago, he was sitting at the kitchen table eating his cereal and reading the obituary column when he came across a name he thought he recognized: J.R. Mooney, beloved husband of Frances, father of Arnold and Paul. He had known Joe Mooney, an accountant for the A&P stores like himself, and he thought his wife's name had been Frances; he remembered Joe had two sons. Usually when he spotted someone he knew, he sent the family a sympathy card, but this time he thought he would pay his respects at the funeral itself. He was to have gone over to Laura and Dick's that day, but at the last minute Laura had called and said they were going to the shore instead and begged him off for another weekend.

Harry arrived at the funeral early and slipped into the back row. There were only fifteen or twenty people there, and he didn't recognize any of them. He watched the family up front. He had no idea that fat Joe Mooney had had such a lovely wife—small and grey-blonde, a fine, frail woman. Harry hadn't known Joe very well; he'd always liked him though. Joe had been an accountant from the Northern New Jersey division, and Joe could make people laugh. Harry had never been able to make people laugh, but he enjoyed a good joke. He used to sit around with the other men, never saying much, but listening to them and to Joe.

He practiced what he would say to Joe's widow. He would tell her: "I knew Joe...not very well, but he always made me laugh." It wasn't until the minister began to deliver the eulogy for Jeffrey Rudolph Mooney—fine husband, loving father, and lifelong worker at Animal and Bird Hospital—that Harry realized he was at the wrong funeral. Yet he was so moved by the eulogy and by the sight of the small, pale widow that he stayed for the whole service. When the widow came out of the chapel, he found himself going up to her and saying, "I knew your husband, and he always made me laugh." The widow stared at him confused, but then she pressed his hands and urged him to come back to the house with their other friends.

As Harry followed the procession to the small frame house on Elm Street, he wondered what more he could say about a man he'd never known, and he wondered why he was following this woman. Yet she seemed so glad to have him come that he didn't want to disappoint her.

Inside the house the widow came up to him right away. She introduced him to her two sons, both tall, imperious men who seemed to Harry to carry themselves a little taller than they were. "So you knew our father?" one of them asked. Harry just nodded. "Are you a veterinarian too?" the other followed up. Harry fumbled with the change in his pocket and glanced around the room. The home was modest like his own, but the furniture was dusty, and he spotted a stray pair of slippers under the couch.

"I'm an accountant," he said. He looked about for a way out of their questions, but the sons stayed with him. Finally he began to negotiate the questions one after the other, and by the end of the afternoon, he felt a flush at how well he'd done. He never lied exactly. He said that once he'd taken his wife's sick cat to Animal and Bird Hospital which was the truth and that he'd met their father there which he decided might have been true. The precariousness of being in a strange house pretending to be somebody he wasn't quite gave him a thrill that afternoon he'd never felt before as though he were opening up new possibilities in himself.

After the Mooney funeral, Harry saw the widow Mooney a few more times. He found he was good at comforting a grieving widow. He listened to her stories about her husband then asked her questions. In return she asked him about his wife. For the first time he was given a chance to talk about his own loss. Up until then no one had really wanted to hear what he felt; his children had avoided the subject as if to spare him and so had his friends. During his first few visits with the widow, he felt a relief. And he felt useful.

Then one evening the widow invited him to her house for a quiet dinner; she stressed "quiet" with a mournful sigh. Harry arrived on time as usual, but the widow wasn't ready. She greeted him at the door in an apron splattered with gravy, and she waved her hands in a fluster at the mess; then she ran to the back of the house to change. Harry went into the kitchen to see if he might help, but what he saw startled him so that he didn't know how to begin. All the cabinets were open, and every pot and pan in the kitchen was out and dirty and stacked on the counters and in the sink. It was a kitchen what would have made Sara cry. The widow came in wearing a black sheath cut a little too low in front and wearing too much perfume. "I hope you like roast beef," she said smiling at Harry, and she pulled a burnt carcass from the oven. "Oh dear," she went on, "I must have mis-set the timer."

"It looks fine," Harry lied, and he took the carcus into the dining room table. Behind him the widow dragged along pots full of potatoes and singed beans and carrots. She spent most of the dinner apologizing for the food and blaming her cooking on her husband's death.

"It's fine, just fine," Harry muttered from time to time, but he could think of nothing more to say to her. He stayed through dinner, and as always he behaved like a gentleman. But he grew tired of hearing about her husband, and he began to wonder what Sara would say about his telling her stories to another woman. Part of him wanted to stay and know this other woman, and yet the wife in him finally retreated.

When the widow called twice the next week, Harry made excuses both times about having to spend the day with his children. Each time after he hung up, he got into his car and drove past his children's houses just so he wouldn't be lying.

After the Mooney funeral, Harry devised some rules for choosing his next widow. He started scanning the obituaries for women with daughters instead of sons, for sons were too concerned over his business connections with their father and were overly protective of their mother. He also looked for a widow of an accountant for such a woman he thought would more likely have the habits he was used to in a wife. And finally, after his second funeral, he added another rule: he would try to find a Jewish widow for a Jewish woman knew how to make a home.

So it was that on the cool blue sky October morning, Harry was reading for the fifth time the notice of Abraham Weiner's funeral. He got up from the table and went into his bedroom. From his closet he took out his grey suit, his grey tie and his black hat. He laid the clothes on the bed the way Sara used to; he placed his black wingtip shoes on the floor. Then he went over to the radio and turned on the morning news and began to dress.

The funeral of Abraham Weiner was a grand event. As Harry drove up in his Dodge, he saw half a dozen black limousines lined in front of the mortuary. For two blocks cars were parked on both sides of the street. Harry almost turned around and started home. Abraham Weiner must have been an important man, he thought, too important for him. But as he was turning in front of the chapel, he glimpsed the widow Weiner being ushered in by another woman. She was looking around at the cars and people as though she were as surprised as he at the importance of the occasion. She was a small woman, dressed in brown tweed with no veil or hat, and Harry thought she looked like a solid, practical woman. He decided to go inside and at least learn who Abraham Weiner was.

Harry sat in the back as usual. There were at least one hundred people at the service, and he wondered if all these people knew and cared for Abraham Weiner. For the first time he began to think about how many people would show up for his funeral, and he could only count eight or ten. Probably there would be more, he thought, but he could rely only on his family, a few friends and perhaps a widow or two. As he sat listening to the readings from the Torah, his own prospects depressed him. Suddenly he felt ashamed for having come to this important man's funeral. He resolved he would leave as soon as the service was over.

When the ceremony finished, he stood with the others to let the family go out first, but as the widow passed him, she stopped suddenly. She put out her hands to him and grasped his. Tears filled her eyes. The family stopped behind her. The congregation strained to see who she had reached for. Harry stood flustered in front of her not knowing what to do. He felt as though he should say something so finally he muttered, "I feel the loss."

"Ah, Jacob, how did you hear?" she asked. She embraced him then and started to cry. Harry stood helpless, but he held her because it seemed the right thing to do.

Finally the younger woman behind her reached out. "We must go now, Mother."

"This is Jacob Levy come back, Rebecca," the widow explained. "After all these years." She took Harry's hand again. "You must come with us," she insisted.

Everything happened so fast that Harry, without knowing exactly how, found himself riding in the back of the head limousine. He had never been in a limousine before. He sat uncomfortably on the jump seat in front of the two women. For them to see him, he had to turn around, and he thought maybe if he never faced them, they wouldn't recognize their mistake.

For the first few miles as the car cruised into the country-side, the widow and her daughter sat in silence. Harry too sat without speaking. He wondered who the widow thought he was. Who was Jacob Levy? At some point he would say to her, "I am Harry Brown, also an accountant, and I have great respect for your husband." (This was the truth, he told himself, for even though he'd never met Abraham Weiner, he respected any man with so many friends.) He tried to relax in his seat. He gazed out on the green New Jersey countryside beginning to blaze into autumn, and he wished his daughter-in-law Laura could see him now riding in the back of a limousine.

Finally Sadie Weiner tapped him on the shoulder. "How did you know, Jacob?" she asked. Harry glanced around. He wanted to tell her who he was, but when he saw her face so open and expectant, he couldn't speak. He looked at her helplessly, and she reached out and patted his hands. "I know. I know," she said. She was a handsome woman with clear skin and deep eyes and a full, expressive mouth. Harry wished for a moment that he were Abraham Weiner or Jacob Levy or someone who knew her. Beside her, her daughter watched him. She was less attractive, a woman of forty, dressed in a shapeless black dress. She seemed only slightly interested in what her mother had to say to him, but she seemed interested in him, Harry thought.

"And how is your father, Jacob?" Sadie Weiner went on. "Is that how you are here...visiting him? The coincidence. I have to think God is watching us."

"There's been a mistake..." Harry said, but as soon as he spoke the words, he wanted to call them back for suddenly he grew afraid that if he announced who he was, he would separate himself from this woman and her daughter;

he would forfeit the possibility of ever being somebody other than himself. And he realized that was what he wanted: to break away and be some other self he hadn't yet discovered.

"You are right, Jacob," Sadie Weiner said. "There has been a terrible, terrible mistake. To have Abraham gone and only now for you to come back. To have all those years in between. Life separates, but we see it also brings together again." She stopped for a minute and considered her words. "If only Abraham knew... but then perhaps it is better he doesn't know. You never understood each other very well." She sighed, a heavy sigh and sat back in her seat where she grew silent once more and stared out the window.

Harry glanced over at her daughter now. Rebecca was watching him from behind black-framed glasses. She had a broad face with a flat nose and the same large mouth of her mother. She could be attractive, Harry thought, but her hair was cut too short and swept away from her face, showing off her worse features. She was large as her father must have been large, and her hips were too wide; but she sat politely, and Harry felt he and she were aligned in some way as an audience to this scene.

When he saw her watching him, Harry glanced down at his lap. He held his hat there with his hands folded over its brim. He grew suddenly conscious of the brown splotches on his hands, and he covered them. Rebecca's hands were young and fair. For the first time Harry found himself wondering what it would be like to have a wife younger than himself.

When the limousine arrived at the Weiner house, friends were already waiting outside. The house was prepared for a funeral with a bowl of water and a towel by the door. The guests were lined up washing their hands of death before entering. The house itself was a large colonial with white columns and grey trim. Harry, Rebecca, and the widow entered by the side door. As the women hurried to their bedrooms to freshen up, Harry was left alone. The house

141

was dark and quiet. It was furnished with heavy European furniture in velvets and brocades. The mirrors were all covered with black cloth; the rooms were lighted by candles in the corners. The house was so still that it seemed to be waiting. For a moment Harry felt as if it were waiting for him.

When the widow and her daughter returned, the three of them formed a receiving line at the door. Harry found himself shaking hands and commiserating with people he'd never seen before. No one knew who he was, but no one asked either. They accepted his place at the side of the family, and they consoled him for his loss. He accepted these condolences as though they were his due. He felt somehow they were. He had never really felt solaced after Sara's death; he had always regretted that not more friends and family had shown up to comfort him.

After all the guests arrived, the widow excused herself and went quickly to her room. Rebecca meanwhile moved off to the kitchen to check on the food, and once again Harry was left alone. He stood in the middle of the hallway uncertain of what to do next. He still held his hat in his hand behind his back. He had been afraid if he set it down someone might find it, and by its shape or size or slightly shoddy brim discover that he was an impostor. All in all he was impressed that he'd handled himself so well. He was thinking how easily he'd slipped into the place of another man when suddenly a voice asked from behind, "Who are you?"

He turned, and he started when he saw Rebecca standing there holding a plate of food. Before he could answer, she went on, "Jacob Levy's been dead for ten years; I've been trying to figure out who you are."

At the news of Jacob Levy's demise, Harry felt a sudden chill run through his body. He started to protest that Jacob Levy couldn't be dead for he was Jacob Levy, but he knew that was absurd. Yet for the last three hours he at least hadn't been Harry Brown...not entirely. He'd fit in; he'd had a place, and he'd been more confident than Harry Brown and a little more caring. But finally he answered, "I'm Harry Brown, an accountant."

Rebecca nodded. "I wondered. You don't look like most of my father's friends."

Harry glanced down at himself, at his boxy grey suit and his out-of-date shoes. All the men in the room were wearing tailored three-piece suits. Suddenly he grew conscious that he was still holding his hat.

Rebecca handed him the plate of food. "I mean no disrespect."

Harry nodded. He took the china plate heaped with whitefish and lox and bagels. He was flattered that she had thought to remember him. He looked around for a place to put his hat, and finally he set it on the hall table.

"You must understand my mother..." Rebecca went on as she led him to a couch in the corner of the living room. "She's been under a great deal of strain. Jacob Levy was my father's business partner twenty years ago. One day he walked out on my father with half the money in the business and never came back. I never knew why, but I always thought it had something to do with my mother. You don't look much like him, at least not to my memory."

Rebecca stared directly at Harry as she talked, and again Harry glanced at the brown spots on his hands; he turned his palms over. "And you certainly don't act like him," she went on. "Jacob Levy was an arrogant bastard...charming, but arrogant. Of course my father was his match, and that was part of the problem."

As Rebecca talked, she kept her arms folded in front of her as if protecting herself or hiding a part of herself. She seemed at ease in this house though Harry could imagine her awkward with people she didn't know and with men. He was taken by her directness, but he felt shy in front of her. He looked at his plate and took a bite of whitefish. The taste stirred memories of his own father and his home.

"I'm an accountant too," she said. Harry noticed the grey flecks in her short black hair. "At my father's firm." He nodded. He was afraid she would now ask him how he knew her father, but she didn't seem to care. "You treated my mother very kindly today, Mr. Brown," she said. "I want

143

to thank you."

Harry shrugged his shoulders. "She is a fine woman."

Rebecca smiled. "At the door I would have sworn you'd been a part of our family for years."

Harry blushed now to remember. "I meant no harm."

Rebecca nodded. "I know that." She stood up from the couch. Suddenly Harry wanted her to stay. He wished he could reach out and touch her. If he'd been Jacob Levy, he wouldn't hesitate, he thought, but Jacob Levy was dead. He strained to find Jacob Levy in himself. He looked around the room. A mirror hung beside them. He wished he could pull off the black cloth and say, "Look here, I'm Harry Brown, and I want you to stay and talk with me."

But Rebecca stopped on her own. "Would you and Mrs. Brown like to come for dinner some time?" she asked. She paused slightly on "Mrs. Brown" as if testing the term. "I think it would do my mother good, and we can explain to her then if we have to who you are."

"There is no Mrs. Brown..." Harry said, "not any more."

"Oh, fine." Rebecca's answer came a little too quickly, and now it was she who flushed.

In the moment of her embarrassment, Harry found his ease. He saw she too was straining to come out of herself. He stood up beside her. She was different than Sara, he thought, smarter, yet less sure of herself. Sara had never questioned who she was. Even on the day she died she was issuing instructions to him on what he should do after she was gone. The problem between him and Sara had always been that he was never sure she needed him. He suspected already that Rebecca Weiner might need him more.

"I mean I'm sorry," she recovered. "But why don't you come yourself."

Harry nodded. "I'd like that, Miss Weiner." He took her hand and held it firmly, yet gently.

"A week from Friday? At eight?" He nodded again. She turned from him then and headed towards the other guests. She moved like a practical, business woman, accepting condolences from friends, offering her own. Harry watched her until she finally went into the other room. Once she glanced back at him. He adjourned to the hallway after that where he found his hat knocked to the floor. He picked it up and left.

On Friday night Harry took his time to dress. He allowed himself a long, hot shower. When he came into his bedroom, he turned on dance music. He had bought a new suit for the evening. He had gone to one of the best men's stores in Morristown and asked the head clerk to fit him. He wanted a suit that was in fashion and one with a little dash. He wanted a vest too and a shirt and tie, shoes, and even socks. He hadn't bought a new suit in six years. Before, when he did buy, Sara had always insisted he go to one of the discount stores for she said their suits were just as good, and they were half the price. As for ties, shirts, socks, Sara had always bought those for him.

The clerk fit Harry in a navy suit with a thin white pin stripe, a powder blue shirt, a navy and red silk tie and black shoes. Harry didn't buy a hat; he wasn't going to wear a hat. His bill for the clothes was seven hundred twenty dollars; he wrote a check. He used Sara's insurance money. She had told him to take a trip with part of the money, to go to Florida or perhaps New Orleans; she had always wanted to go to New Orleans. She told him not to tell anyone how much money he'd gotten, not even the children. Otherwise people would start coming around expecting things, she said. But on the way home from the clothes store, Harry bought presents for his grandchildren—electric train sets and doll houses. For Susie and Bill he bought a dishwasher and for Laura and Dick, new patio furniture. He bought large presents, not token gifts, things he knew they wanted. Harry wanted people to expect things from him from now on. He needed them to expect things.

As Harry put on his new clothes, he paused to feel the soft cotton of his shirt and the fine weave of the wool in his suit. Adjusting his tie in the mirror, he studied himself. So Jacob Levy was an arrogant bastard, he said out loud.

Well, he, Harry Brown was not arrogant, and he had fit in as Harry Brown, confident, caring Harry Brown. He didn't know if he would tell Rebecca tonight that he had never known her father, but somehow he thought it might not matter. He would tell her perhaps in a few weeks when he invited her to meet Laura and Dick and Susie and Bill and his grandchildren.